"I've changed my mind."

Eva stopped in front of Kyle. Any nerves about seducing him had long since burned away. She ran a finger down his chest, igniting a trail of heat. The heady masculine scents of clean skin and sandalwood made her head spin.

His hand curled over hers. "What about?"

She boldly wound one arm around his neck, leaned in close and gently bit down on one earlobe. "The clause in our marriage agreement that prohibits sex. If anyone is going to sleep with my husband, it's going to be me."

When she would have drawn back, his hands closed on her waist, holding her against him. "I'll get my lawyer to strike it out in the morning."

"As long as we have a verbal agreement, the new condition is in effect."

"We could shake on it," he muttered, "but I have a better idea." Lowering his head, he finally did what she'd been dying for him to do ever since the wedding ceremony. He kissed her.

* * *

Needed: One Convenient Husband
is part of The Pearl House series—
Business and passion collide when two dynasties
forge ties bound by love

Dear Reader,

Eva is a heroine who has simmered in the background of other Pearl House books, almost too interesting to have around, because she is gorgeous, assertive and has issues. One of them is that she doesn't want to marry, ever. Too bad that when her adoptive father, Mario Atraeus, dies, the will states she has to marry, or else...

It was fun and interesting to write Eva and Kyle's story. When you think about it, a marriage-of-convenience conflict is so fraught. Who would want to be married to someone they don't love? Added to that, both Eva and Kyle carried scars when it came to relationships.

Getting them together was like trying to mix oil and water. Luckily for Eva and Kyle, they had an irresistible attraction for each other that proved unexpectedly healing. And I guess that's why I write these books. Love has a power that transcends. It transforms people and relationships and situations, no matter how scarred.

I hope you enjoy,

Fiona Brand

NEEDED:
ONE CONVENIENT
HUSBAND

—

FIONA BRAND

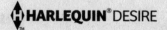

HARLEQUIN® DESIRE

ISBN-13: 978-0-373-73443-6

Needed: One Convenient Husband

Copyright © 2016 by Fiona Gillibrand

Never Too Late
Copyright © 2006 by Harlequin Books S.A.
Brenda Jackson is acknowledged as the author of this work.

Recycling programs
for this product may
not exist in your area.

Printed in U.S.A.

CONTENTS

Fiona Brand lives in the sunny Bay of Islands, New Zealand. Now that both her sons are grown, she continues to love writing books and gardening. After a life-changing time in which she met Christ, she has undertaken study for a bachelor of theology and has become a member of The Order of St. Luke, Christ's healing ministry.

Books by Fiona Brand

Harlequin Desire

The Sheikh's Pregnancy Proposal

The Pearl House series

A Breathless Bride
A Tangled Affair
A Perfect Husband
The Fiancée Charade
Just One More Night
Needed: One Convenient Husband

Harlequin Romantic Suspense

O'Halloran's Lady

Silhouette Romantic Suspense

Cullen's Bride
Heart of Midnight
Blade's Lady
Marrying McCabe
Gabriel West: Still the One
High-Stakes Bride

Visit her Author Profile page at
Harlequin.com for more titles!

NEEDED:
ONE CONVENIENT
HUSBAND
Fiona Brand

For the Lord. Thank You.

I am the light of the world.
Whoever follows me will never walk in darkness,
but will have the light of life.

—*John* 8:12

One

Kyle Messena's gaze narrowed as the bridal car pulled up outside Dolphin Bay's windblown, hilltop church. The bride, festooned in white tulle, stepped out of the limousine. A drift of gauze obscured her face, but sunlight gleamed on tawny hair that was heart-stoppingly familiar.

Adrenaline pumped and time seemed to slow, stop, as he considered the stunning fact that, despite his efforts to prevent Eva Atraeus marrying a man whose motives were purely financial, she had utterly fooled him and the wedding he had thought he had nixed was going ahead.

Kyle had taken two long, gliding steps out of the inky shade cast by an aged oak into the blistering heat of a New Zealand summer's day before the ocean breeze whipped the veil from the bride's face.

It wasn't Eva.

Relief unlocked the fierce tension that gripped him. A tension that sliced through the indifference to relationships that had shrouded him for years, ever since the death of his wife and small son. Deaths that he should have prevented.

The unwanted, brooding intensity had grown over the months he had been entrusted with the duty of ensuring that the heiress to an Atraeus fortune married according to a draconian clause in her adoptive father's will. Eva, in order to get control of her inheritance, had to either marry a Messena—*him*—or a man who genuinely wanted her and not her money.

Acting as Eva's trustee did not sit well with Kyle. He was aware that his wily great-uncle, Mario, had named him as trustee in a last game-playing move to maneuver him into marrying the woman he had once wanted but left behind. Confronted by the mesmerizing power of an attraction that still held him in reluctant thrall and unable to accept that the one woman he had never been able to forget would marry someone else, Kyle had been unable to refuse the job.

A gust of wind whipped the bride's veil to one side, revealing that she was a little on the plump side. Her hair was also a couple of shades lighter than the rich dark mane shot through with tawny highlights that had been a natural feature of Eva's hair ever since he'd first set eyes on her at age sixteen.

Kyle's jaw unlocked. Now that he had successfully circumvented Eva's latest marriage plan, he was ready to leave, but when a zippy white sports car emblazoned with the name of Eva's business, Perfect Weddings, pulled into a space, Kyle knew he wasn't going anywhere.

Eva Atraeus, dressed in a pale pink button-down suit that clung in all the right places, closed the door with an expensive *thunk*. Cell held to one ear, she hooked a matching pale pink tote over her shoulder and started to-

ward the church doors, her stride fluid and distractingly
sexy in a pair of strappy high heels. At five feet seven,
Eva was several inches too short for the runway, but with
her elegant, curvy figure, mouthwatering cheekbones
and exotic dark eyes, she had been a knockout success
as a photographic model. Gorgeous, quirky and certifi-
ably high maintenance, Eva had fascinated gossip columnists for years and dazzled more men than she'd had
hot dinners, including *him*.

Every muscle in Kyle's body tightened on a visceral
hit of awareness that had become altogether too familiar.

A faint check in her step indicated that Eva had spot-
ted him.

As the bridal party disappeared into the church, she
terminated her call and changed direction. Stepping beneath the shade of the oak, she shoved the cell in her tote
and glared at him. "What are you doing at *my* wedding?"

Kyle clamped down on his irritation at Eva's delib-
erate play on the "my wedding" bit. It was true that it
was supposed to have been her actual wedding day. Un-
derstandably, she was annoyed that he'd upset her plan
to leverage a marriage of convenience by offering the
groom a lucrative job in Dubai. The way Kyle saw it, he
had simply countered one employment opportunity with
another. The fact that Jeremy, an accountant, had taken
the job so quickly and had even seemed relieved, more
than justified his intervention. "You shouldn't have arranged a wedding you knew couldn't go ahead."

Her dark gaze flashed. "What if I was in love with
Jeremy?"

He lifted a brow. "After a whole four weeks?"

"You know as well as I that it can happen a whole lot
faster than—" She stopped, her cheeks flushed. Rum-
maging in her bag, she found sunglasses and, with con-

trolled precision, slipped them onto the bridge of her nose. "Now you get to tell me what you're doing at a *private* wedding. I'm guessing it's not just to have another argument."

He crossed his arms over his chest. "If you think you can kick me out, forget it. I'm a guest of the groom. I manage his share portfolio."

She took a deep breath and he watched with objective fascination as the flare of irritation was replaced by one of the gorgeous smiles that had graced magazines and posters and which had the power to stop all male brain function. "That's thin, even for you."

"But workable."

"And here I was thinking you were here to make sure I hadn't pulled off a last-minute coup and found another groom."

He frowned at the light, floral waft of her perfume and resisted the impulse to step a little closer. "It's not my brief to stop you marrying."

Her head tilted to one side. Through the screen of the lenses her gaze chilled. "No, it's to stop me marrying the man of my choice."

"You need to choose better." Out of an impressive discard pile during the last few months, on three different occasions, Eva had selected a prospective groom. Unfortunately, all three had been strapped for cash and willing to sign prenuptial agreements that spelled out the cutoff date for the marriage: two years to the day, the exact time period specified in Mario's will. Kyle had been honorbound by the terms of the will to veto the weddings.

"Jeremy was perfect husband material. He was attractive, personable, with a reasonable job, his—"

"Motive was blatantly financial."

Her expression turned steely. "He needed money to cover some debts. What is so wrong with that?"

"Mario would spin in his grave if you married a man with a gambling addiction."

There was a small icy silence, intensified by the strains of the wedding march emanating from the church. "If I have to marry Mr. Right according to Kyle Messena, then maybe *you* should choose someone for me. Only I'll need to marry him by—" she checked the slim pink watch on her wrist "—next month. Since now, thanks to you, I only have three weeks left to marry before my inheritance goes into lockdown for the next *thirteen years*."

Despite Kyle's resolve to withstand the considerable pressure he had always known Eva would apply, a twinge of guilt made his stomach tighten.

Women and relationships in general had always proved to be a difficult area for him. It was a fact that he was more comfortable with the world of military operations or the clinical cut and thrust of his family's banking business. He could do weapons and operational tactics; he could do figures and financial markets. Love and the responsibility—and the searing guilt that came with it—was something he would not risk again. "It isn't my intention to prevent you getting your inheritance."

Eva's serene smile disappeared. "No," she said with a throaty little catch to her voice. "It's just turning out that way."

Spinning on her heel, Eva marched back to her car.

Kyle frowned. Eva's voice had sounded suspiciously husky, as if she was on the verge of tears. In the entire checkered history of their relationship, he had only ever seen Eva, who was superorganized with a serene, kick-ass calm, cry twice. Of course, she had cried at Mario's funeral almost a year ago. The only other occasion had been close on eleven years ago when he'd been nineteen. To be precise, it had been the morning after Mario had hauled them both over the coals for a passionate interlude on Dolphin Bay's beach.

Memory flickered. A hot, extended twilight, a buttery moon sliding up over the sea, the clamor of a family party at the resort fading in the distance as Eva had wound her arms around his neck. He'd drawn a deep breath, caught the scent of her hair, her skin. Every muscle had tensed as he'd dipped his head and given in to the temptation that had kept him in agony most of the summer and kissed her...

If Mario hadn't come looking for Eva, they would have done a lot more than just kiss. The interview with Mario that had ensued that night had been sharp and short. As gorgeous and put-together as Eva had looked at age seventeen, she had more than her share of vulnerabilities. The product of a severely dysfunctional family, Eva needed security and protection, not seduction. Mario hadn't elaborated on any of those details, but the message had been plain enough. Eva was off-limits.

Until now.

He had no illusions about why Mario had done a complete about turn and made him a trustee, when for years he had treated Kyle as if he was a marauding predator after his one and only chick. For years Eva had stubbornly resisted Mario's attempts to find her a safe, solid husband from amongst the sons of his wealthy business associates. Mario, forced to change tack, had swallowed his objections to the "wild Messena boys," and had then tried to marry Eva off to both of Kyle's older brothers, Gabriel and Nick. When that strategy had failed because Gabe and Nick had married other women and Kyle's younger brother Damian had a long-standing girlfriend, in a last desperate move, Mario had finally settled on Kyle as a prospective bridegroom.

His gaze still locked on Eva, Kyle strolled back to his Maserati. Now that he knew Eva wasn't the bride, he should drive back to Auckland. Back to his ultrabusy, smoothly organized life. If he left right away, he could even make the uncomplicated dinner date he had with Elise, a fellow banking executive he had been seeing on and off for the past few months, mostly at business functions.

But as he approached the Maserati, which was nose to tail with Eva's white sports car, he couldn't shake the sense that something about the way Eva had stormed off had not rung true. It occurred to him that the tears he thought Eva had been about to cry could have been fake. After all, she *had* taken acting classes. She had been good enough that she had even been offered a part in a popular soap, but had turned it down because it had conflicted with her desire to start her own wedding planning business.

Suddenly positive that he had been duped, he dropped the Maserati's key back into his pocket. There could be only one reason why Eva wanted him to feel guilty enough that he bypassed the reception. She had already found a new candidate for groom and he would be attending as her guest. Since she only had three weeks to organize her final shot at a wedding, keeping her new prospective groom close made sense, because time was of the essence.

Certainty settled in when he caught the tail end of a conversation with someone named Troy. His jaw tightened. Troy Kendal, if he didn't miss his guess. A flashy sports star Eva had met less than a week ago in a last, desperate attempt to recruit a groom. Out of nowhere, the jealousy he had worked hard to suppress because it was just as illogical as the desire that haunted him, roared to life.

If Eva had been crying, they had been crocodile tears.

She had been getting rid of him.

In no mood to leave now, Kyle waited until Eva terminated the call and dropped the phone in her bag. "We need to talk."

"I thought we just did."

Dropping her bag on the passenger seat, she dragged off her sunglasses and checked her watch, subtly underlining the fact that she was in a hurry to leave. Without the barrier of the lenses, and with strands of hair blowing loose around her cheeks, she seemed younger and oddly vulnerable, although Kyle knew that was an illusion, since Eva's reputation with men was legendary. "There's a solution to your problem. If you marry a Messena, there are no further conditions, other than that the marriage must be of two years' duration."

Her brows creased as if she was only just considering an option that had been bluntly stated in the will. "Even if I wanted to do that, which I don't, that's hardly possible, since Gabriel and Nick are both married, and Damian's as good as."

Kyle's jaw clamped at the systematic way she ticked his brothers off her fingers, deliberately leaving him off the list. *As if her fingers had never locked with his as they'd strolled down the dimly lit path to Dolphin Bay, as if she had never wrapped her arms around his neck and kissed him.*

"There's one other Messena," Kyle said flatly, his patience gone. "I'm talking you, me and a marriage of convenience."

Two

Eva choked back the stinging refusal she wanted to fling at Kyle. She didn't know why she reacted so strongly to him or the idea that they could marry. Mario's previous attempts to marry her off to other Messena men had barely ruffled her.

A year ago, when she had read the terms of the will and absorbed the full import of that one little sentence, she had been so horrified she had wanted to crawl under the solicitor's desk and hide. The whole idea that Kyle, the only available Messena husband—and the one man who had ditched her—should feel pressured to marry her, had been mortifying. "I don't need a pity proposal."

The wind dropped for a split second, enclosing them in a pooling, tension-filled silence that was gradually filled with the timeless beauty of the wedding vows floating from the church.

"But you do need *a* proposal. After two years, once

you've got your inheritance, we can dissolve the marriage."

Kyle's clinical solution contrarily sent a stab of hurt through her, which annoyed her intensely.

A former Special Air Service soldier, Kyle had the kind of steely blue gaze that missed nothing. He was also tall and muscular, six foot two inches of sleek muscle, with close-cut dark hair and the kind of grim good looks and faintly battered features, courtesy of his years in the military, that mesmerized women.

All of the men in the Messena and Atraeus families seemed to possess that same formidable, in-charge quality. Usually, it didn't ruffle her in the slightest, but Kyle paired it with a blunt, low-key insight that was unnerving; he seemed to know what she was going to do before she did it. Added to that, she wouldn't mind betting that he had gotten rid of some of her grooms with a little judicious intimidation.

The idea of marrying Kyle shouldn't affect her. She had learned early on to sidestep actual relationships at all cost. The plain fact was, she wouldn't have trusted in any relationships at all if it hadn't been for Mario and his wife picking her up when they'd found her on the sidewalk near their home one evening twelve years ago.

When they'd found out she was on the run from her last home because her foster father had wandering hands, they had phoned the welfare people. However, instead of allowing her to be shunted back into another institutional home, Mario had made a string of phone calls to "people he knew" and she had been allowed to stay with them.

Despite her instinctive withdrawal and the cold neutrality that had gotten her through a number of foster homes, Mario and Teresa had offered her the kind of quiet, steady love that, at sixteen, had been unfamiliar and a little scary. When they had eventually proposed adopting her, the plain fact was she hadn't known how to respond. She'd had the rug pulled emotionally so many times she had thought that if she softened and believed that she was deserving of love, that would be the moment it was all taken away.

In the end, through Mario's dogged persistence, she had finally understood that he was the one person who wouldn't break his word. Her resistance had crumbled and she had signed. In the space of a moment, she had ceased to be Eva Rushton, the troubled runaway, and had become Eva Atraeus, a member of a large and mystifyingly welcoming family.

However, the transformation had never quite been complete. After watching her own mother's three marriages disintegrate then at age seventeen finding out *why*, she had decided she did not ever want to be that vulnerable.

She caught a whiff of Kyle's cologne and her stomach clenched. And there was her problem, she thought grimly. Although, why the fiery tension, which should have died a death years ago—right after he had dumped her when she was seventeen—still persisted, she had no clue. It wasn't as if they had ever spent much time together or had anything in common beyond the youthful attraction. Kyle had married someone else a couple of years later, too, so she knew that what they had shared had not affected him as deeply as it had her.

Now, thanks to Kyle's interference, she had three weeks to marry anyone but him, and the clock was ticking…

Frustration reignited the nervous tension that had assaulted her when Jeremy had informed her he was backing out of their arrangement, but now that tension was laced with a healthy jolt of panic. Mario Atraeus couldn't have chosen a better watchdog for the unexpected codicil he had written into his will if he had tried.

She had been so close to marriage, but now Jeremy had run like a frightened rabbit. She couldn't prove that Kyle had engineered the job offer to get rid of Jeremy. All she knew was that he had used the same tactic twice before. Every time she got someone to agree to marry her, Kyle got rid of him.

Although why Kyle had stopped her marrying a man who had been eminently suitable, and whom she had actually liked in a lukewarm kind of way, she didn't know. Given their antagonistic past, she had thought Kyle would have been only too glad to discharge a responsibility that had been thrust on him, and which he could not possibly want.

Just like he hadn't wanted her.

Frowning at the thought of the brief, passionate interlude they had shared eleven years ago, she met Kyle's gaze squarely. "Thanks, but no thanks."

Dropping into the little sports car's bucket seat, she snapped the door closed. The engine revved with a throaty roar. Throat tight, still unbearably ruffled that he had actually had the gall to give her a *pity* proposal, she put the car in gear. Spinning the car in a tight turn, she headed in the direction of the Dolphin Bay Resort, where the reception was being held.

Her jaw tightened at the thought that even the location of the reception was tainted with memories of Kyle and the one time he'd kissed her. In starting her wedding business, though, she'd had to be pragmatic. The Dolphin Bay Resort was family run and offered her a great discount. She would have been flat-out stupid not to use the venue.

Still fuming, Eva strolled into the resort to oversee the gorgeous, high-end fairy-tale wedding she had designed as a promotional centerpiece for her wedding planning business. A perfect wedding that should have been hers, if only Jeremy hadn't cut and run.

Cancel that, she thought grimly. If only Kyle hadn't paid Jeremy off with a lucrative job offer in sandblasted Dubai! Taking a deep breath and reaching for her usual calm control, she checked her appearance in one of the elegant mirrors that decorated the walls. The reflection that bounced back was reassuring. Lately her emotions were all over the place, she was crying at the drop of a hat, she actually wanted to watch rom-coms and she was having trouble sleeping.

None of that inner craziness showed. She looked as calm and cool and collected as she wished she felt, her mass of tawny hair smoothed into an elegant French pleat, her too curvy figure disguised by a low-key skirt and jacket in a pastel pink that matched her shoes and handbag. The businesslike but feminine image achieved a balance between the occasion and her role as planner.

More importantly, it ensured that she did not compete with the bride or other female guests in any way. She had learned that lesson at what would have been her first wedding when the groom had gotten a little too interested in her and the bride had cancelled.

Eva walked through to the ballroom where the reception was being held and lifted a hand to acknowledge the waitstaff, all of whom she knew well thanks to the half dozen weddings she had staged at Dolphin Bay. She tensed as she glimpsed commiseration in the normally businesslike gaze of the maître d' as he mopped around an ice sculpture of swans she had recklessly commissioned because this was supposed to be her one and only wedding day.

The five-tiered extravaganza of a cake, snow-white

icing sparkling with crystals and festooned with clusters of sculpted flowers so beautifully executed they looked real, stopped her brisk movement through the room. Out of the blue, the emotion she had been working hard to stamp out grabbed at her. She had wanted to make this a day she would remember all of her life. Unfortunately, that had been achieved since it would be difficult to forget that her perfect wedding now belonged to someone else.

Stomach churning with a potent cocktail of frustration, panic and a crazy vulnerability caused by the fact that Kyle seemed intent on stopping her attempts to achieve a workable, safe marriage, she spun on her heel and made a beeline for the kitchen.

Bracing herself, she pushed the double doors open and stepped into a hive of gleaming white walls and polished steel counters. The cheerful clattering and hum of conversation instantly stopped. Eva's chest squeezed tight as waves of sympathy flowed toward her, intensifying the ache that had started in her throat and making tears burn at the back of her eyes. The jolt of emotion was crazy, given that she hadn't loved Jeremy in the least and marriage had not been on her horizon until Mario had literally forced her to it with that clause in his will. A clause designed to railroad her into the kind of happiness he had shared with his wife and which he had thought she should also have, whether she wanted it or not.

Until she'd started planning this wedding, she had thought Mario had been utterly wrong in believing he could make her want to be married. But every detail of planning her own wedding had confronted her, throwing together the stark realities of her life and cruelly highlighting the parts she couldn't have: the romance and the happy-ever-after ending that true love promised. Most of all, it emphasized the happy aftermath she would never experience: her own babies.

She had known since she was seventeen, thanks to a rare genetic disorder she carried, that she shouldn't have children. The disorder had proved fatal for her twin and two siblings, which had made her doubly wary about the whole concept of marriage. There was always the possibility that she could meet someone who didn't care about the disorder and who would be happy to adopt, but she had difficulty getting past the fact that she literally carried death in her genes.

In retrospect, it had been a huge mistake giving in to the temptation to design a wedding that patently did not go with a marriage of convenience. It smacked of wish fulfilment, and it had opened up a Pandora's box of needs and desires she had thought she had put behind her. She should have settled for a registry office ceremony. No fuss, no bother, no emotion.

Pinning a smile on her face, she breezed through the large bustling kitchen and waved at the head chef, Jerome, a Parisian with two Michelin stars. Jerome had designed the menu personally for her. He sent her an intense look brimming with passionate outrage and sympathy, even though he knew she had managed to sell the wedding on to a couple who had been desperate to marry quickly, owing to a surprise pregnancy.

Eva flinched at the concept that her pretty young bride not only had her perfect wedding, but was also pregnant. She could not afford to dwell on the painful issue that while she could not have children, other women could, and at the drop of a hat.

Keeping her professional smile firmly fixed, Eva fished her menu out of her bag and ran through it with Jerome. For once there were no last-minute glitches. Every aspect of this wedding appeared to be abnormally perfect. After dutifully admiring the exquisite mountain of cupcakes, which Jerome was decorating—her favorite forbidden snack—she escaped back to the reception room before he could toss his icing palette knife down and pull her into a comforting bear hug.

Kyle had proposed.

The kitchen doors made a swishing sound as they swung closed behind her. Eva stared blindly at the crisp white damask on the tables, the sparkle of crystal chandeliers and lavish clusters of white roses. She did not know why Kyle had the power to upset her so. It wasn't as if she was immersed in the painful, oversentimental first love that had gripped her at age seventeen. It wasn't as if she still wanted him.

As the wedding guests began to spill through the doors, she rummaged in her handbag, found and slipped on a pair of the most unflattering glasses she'd been able to buy. The lenses were fake, just plain glass, but the heavy, dark rims served to deflect the attention that her good looks usually attracted.

Fixing a smile on her face, she did a brisk circuit of the main reception room, which she and her assistant, Jacinta, had dressed earlier. Waiters were loading silver trays with flutes filled with extremely good champagne she had sourced from an organic vineyard. Trays of her favorite canapés from the five-star kitchen were lined up in the servery.

The reception was heartbreakingly gorgeous. Since it was supposed to have been her own, she had put a great deal of thought into every detail, no expense spared. The only consolation was that she would be very well paid. And, in three weeks' time, if she was still unwed, she would be in desperate need of cash in order to retain her house and keep her business afloat.

The doors to the kitchens behind her swished open as guests began to seat themselves at tables. Jacinta Doyle, her sleekly efficient personal assistant, came to stand beside her, a folder in one hand. Jacinta gave her a look laden with sympathy but, tactfully, kept things business-like. Halfway through a list of minor details, she stopped dead. "*Who* is that?"

An annoying hum of awareness Eva was desperate to ignore made her tense. Adjusting the glasses, which were too heavy for her nose, she frowned at the rapidly filling room. Her mood plummeted when she saw Kyle. "Who do you mean, exactly? There must be a hundred people in the room."

"He is *hot*." Jacinta, who was hooked into the sophisticated, very modern dating scene with a new man on her arm every week, clutched dramatically at her chest before pointing Kyle out just in case Eva hadn't noticed him. "I'm in love."

Irritation flared, instant and unreasoning. "I thought you were dating Geraldo someone-or-other."

"Gerard. His visa ran out, and his money." She shrugged. "He went back to France."

Eva pretended to be absorbed in her own checklist of things to do. "Don't let your heart beat faster over Kyle, because you'll be wasting your time. He's too old for you, and he's not exactly a fun type."

"How old?"

The irritation morphed into something else she couldn't quite put her finger on. "Thirty," she muttered shortly.

"I wouldn't call that old. More…interesting."

Something inside Eva snapped. "Forget Kyle Messena. He isn't available."

Jacinta sent her a glance laced with the kind of curiosity that informed Eva she hadn't been able to keep the sharpness out of her voice. "Kyle Messena. I thought he looked familiar. Didn't he lose his wife and child in some kind of terrorist attack overseas? But that was years ago." She pointedly returned her gaze to Kyle, underlining the fact that she could look at him any time she liked, for as long as she liked.

Even more annoyed by the speculation on Jacinta's face, as if she was actually considering making a play for Kyle, Eva consulted her watch. "We're ten minutes behind schedule," she said crisply. "You check the timing for service with the chef. I'm going to get a cold drink then have a word with the musicians. With any luck we'll get out of here before midnight."

With a last glance at Kyle, Jacinta closed the folder with a resigned snap. "No problem."

But there was a problem, Eva thought bleakly. The kind of problem she had never imagined she would suffer from ever again. For reasons she did not understand, Jacinta's interest in Kyle had evoked the kind of fierce, primitive response she had only ever experienced once before, years ago, when she'd heard that Kyle was dating someone else.

She needed to go somewhere quiet and give herself a stern talking-to, because somehow, she had allowed the unwanted attraction to Kyle to get out of hand, to the point that she was suddenly, burningly, crazily jealous about the last man she wanted in her life.

Three

Kyle strolled to the bar, although if he were honest, the drive to get a cold beer over settling for the champagne being served had more to do with the fact that Eva was headed in that direction.

Eva's expression chilled as he leaned on the bar next to her. The faint crease in her smooth brow as she sipped from a tall glass of what he guessed was sparkling water somehow made her look even more spectacularly gorgeous, despite the disfiguring glasses. It was a beauty he should have been accustomed to, yet it still made his stomach tighten and his attention sharpen in a completely male way.

She met his gaze briefly before looking away. An impression of defensiveness made him frown. Normally Eva was cool and distant, occasionally combative, but never defensive.

She placed the glass down on the counter with a small click. "I thought you had left."

The unspoken words, *now that you'd made sure I hadn't secretly gotten married*, seemed to hang in the air. Kyle shrugged and ordered a beer. "I decided to stick around. We still need to have a conversation."

"If it's about the terms of the will, forget it. I've read the fine print—"

"You've ignored the fine print." She had certainly failed to notice that he was her primary marriage candidate.

The faint blush of color in her cheeks flared a little brighter, sharpening Kyle's curiosity. Eva was behaving in a way that was distinctly odd. He was abruptly certain that something had happened, something had changed, although he had no idea what.

She sent him a breezy professional smile, but her whole demeanor was evasive. "If you don't mind, I really do need to work."

Usually, Eva was as direct and uncompromising as any man. The blush and the avoidance of eye contact didn't fit, unless… His heart slammed against his chest, spinning him back to the long summer days they had spent on the beach as teenagers. For a split second he wondered that he had missed something so obvious. But he guessed he had been so absorbed with trying to control the desire that had come out of left field that he had failed to see that Eva was fighting the same battle.

She tried to sidestep him, but the bar area was now filling up with people, lining up for drinks. Feeling like a villain, but riveted by the discovery, he moved slightly, just enough to block her in. She stopped, a bare inch from brushing against his chest.

Kyle's stomach tightened as he caught another whiff of Eva's perfume. He knew he should leave her alone and let her get on with her job. But the desire to evoke a response, to make Eva admit that she wanted him, was too strong. "The whole point of Mario's will was that he wanted you to marry someone who would actually care about you and who wasn't in it for the money."

"I know what Mario wanted, no one better. What I don't get is why you're so intent on enforcing a condition that is patently ridiculous?"

Kyle's gaze narrowed at the way Eva carefully avoided the issue of his proposal. "You're family."

"Distant and only on paper. It's not as if I'm a real Atraeus."

Kyle's brow's jerked together. "Your name is Atraeus."

Eva dragged in a breath, relieved that the unnerving sense that Kyle had seen right through her desperate attempt to seem normal and completely impervious to him had dissipated. "That doesn't change the fact that I'm adopted. I'm not blood." And that she could still remember what it felt like to wear secondhand clothes, eat cereal for dinner and fend off her mother's boyfriends. She was a very poor cuckoo in a diamond-encrusted nest.

"Mario wanted to help you. He wanted you to be happy."

She drew a breath. The clean scent of his skin deepened the panicked awareness that was humming through her. "I'm twenty-eight. I think that by now I know what it takes to be happy."

"And that would be paying some guy to marry you?"

Eva's brows jerked together. "Correct me if I'm wrong, but barely fifty years ago, arranged marriages were common in both the Messena and the Atraeus families."

"Last century, maybe."

"Then someone should have told that to Mario. And it underlines my point that a marriage of convenience is not the worst thing that could happen." And it wasn't as if she actually wanted to be loved. She had seen what had happened to her mother when she had become emotionally needy. Relationship train wreck followed by train wreck, the plunging depression and slow disintegration of Meg Rushton's life. It had all been crowned by her mother's inability to care for Eva, the one child who had survived the disorder.

A young man tried to squeeze in beside Eva. Kyle blocked him with a wolf-cold glance and a faint shift in position. In the process, his arm brushed against hers, sending a tingle of heat through her that made Eva even more desperate to get away. With grim concentration, she stared over Kyle's broad shoulder at the bottles of spirits suspended at the rear of the bar and tried not to love the fact that Kyle's behavior had been as bluntly possessive as if they had been a couple. That was exactly the kind of thinking she could not afford.

Kyle's gaze, edged with irritation, captured hers. "Let's put this in context. If a man is unscrupulous enough to take your money for marriage, chances are he won't have a problem pressurizing you until you give in to sex."

Eva's heart thumped hard in her chest at the thought that Kyle could possibly have a motivation that was tied in with caring about her, that in his own hard-nosed way, he had been trying to protect her. The next thought was a dizzying, improbable leap—that Kyle had a personal interest in stopping her from having sex with other men because *he* wanted her.

Annoyed that she should even begin to imagine that Kyle's concern was based on some kind of personal desire for her when she knew he regarded her as a spoiled, shallow good-time girl, she put the revelation in context. Kyle was gorgeous, megawealthy and successful, but the reality was that, like his older brothers and her macho

Atraeus cousins, shunt him back a few centuries, give him a sword and buckler and he would fit right in. Just because he was being protective to the point of being intrusive didn't mean he was attracted to her. It was just part of his DNA. "I know how to handle men. Believe me, sex will not be an issue."

Kyle's gaze dropped to her mouth. "Then, honey, you don't know men very well."

Her heart pounded a little harder, not at the implication that she was naive about men in general, but at the low, rough timbre of his voice and the sudden revelation that Kyle *did* find her attractive.

Eva swallowed against the sudden dryness in her throat. The fingers of her right hand curled tight against the childish urge to press the heel of her palm against the sharp pounding of her heart.

Someone else jostled her to get to the bar. Kyle said something low and curt, his arm curled around her waist as he pulled her against his side. The move was more courteous and protective than overtly sensual, but even so, another hot pang shot clear to her toes.

He released her almost immediately, but not before his gaze touched on hers, filled with unexpected knowledge. Another shockwave went through her. If she'd thought Kyle hadn't noticed that she was still crazily attracted to him, she was wrong. He knew.

"Damn, let's get out of here."

Taking her hand, he forged a path through the now-busy bar, and out of the blue, memories she'd buried flooded back. Kyle's fingers linked with hers years ago, the carefree flash of his grin as they'd escaped from the crowded party. The way the earth had stopped spinning and she'd forgotten to breathe when they had run down to the beach and long weeks of swimming and talking together had finally reached a flash point.

Breath suddenly constricted, she pulled her hand free and tried to ignore the heated tingling of the brief contact.

Kyle stopped, coincidentally, right beside the wedding cake. "You might think you can handle marriage to some guy you've only just met, but I know for a fact you've never even lived with a man."

The memories winked out with the suddenness of a door slamming. Her temper flared at the evidence that Kyle had been prying into her life. "Just because I haven't had a long-term relationship—"

"The way I heard it, you haven't had *any* real relationships."

She dragged off the glasses, her eyes flashing fire. "How can you know this stuff?" Although she knew the answer had to be Kyle's younger sisters, the Messena twins, Sophie and Francesca. Over the years she had become good friends with the twins, so of course they knew exactly how her life had played out. No doubt Kyle had engaged Sophie and Francesca in some kind of casual conversation, *gathering intelligence*. They would not have realized that telling Kyle she didn't go in for casual relationships would matter. "I knew it. You've been *spying* on me."

"Checking up on you. It's part of the brief."

And with his military background, Kyle had a certain skill set. When he had gone into the army, she had still been lovesick enough to keep tabs on him. Not satisfied with the rank and file, he had done officer training, then had gone into the Special Air Service, the SAS. When he had been sent on his first overseas assignment, she had lost sleep for weeks, wondering if he had been wounded or even killed. Then she had learned that he had come back from the mission just fine and gotten married on his days off. It was then she had decided she would never worry about him again.

She folded her arms across her chest, glad to have that salutary reminder about just how meaningless that long-ago holiday romance and kiss on the beach had been. "I am not a job."

"No." He stared at the monster cake with a faintly incredulous gaze. "You're a pain in the butt."

Her chin shot up. "Then why do the job?"

"Believe me, if Mario had chosen someone else, I would have been more than happy."

"Ditto."

A muscle jerked fascinatingly along the side of his jaw. Bolstered by the unmistakable sign of tension, Eva delivered the only ultimatum she had. "Then unless you want to keep tabs on me for the next thirteen years as my trustee, maybe you should let me get on with the business of getting married."

"Troy Kendal will never marry you."

She should have been shocked by the flat pronouncement, but in a weird way, after the relentless research he had conducted into all of her other grooms, she had half expected him to find out. "You don't know that."

The resolute quality of his gaze, as if he would let her marry Troy over his dead body, sent a forbidden little thrill through her. She drew a breath in an effort to still the rapid pounding of her heart. Something was definitely, seriously wrong with her. She should have been angry, desperate. She shouldn't *like* it that Kyle was systematically getting rid of her grooms.

She slid her glasses back onto the bridge of her nose, suddenly needing the camouflage. "This conversation is over. I have a business to run."

Kyle dragged his gaze from the mesmerizing sight of Eva walking away, gripping her official clipboard. His frown deepened when he noted a familiar figure giving him the kind of narrowed, assessing stare he had gotten used to over the past few months. Kendal was new on the list of men Eva had dated since Mario had died. He also deviated from the pattern of older, biddable admirers Eva had approached in order to find a manageable, paid husband.

Kendal was twenty-four, which made him younger than Eva by four years. He was also a well-known professional rugby player with a list of stormy liaisons behind him. Recently, Kendal had been sidelined by injury and had missed the cut for the new season, which meant his career was stalled. According to the research Kyle had done, he was also currently strapped for cash.

His jaw tightened as Kendal slung his arm around Eva's waist. He knew exactly where and when Eva had picked Kendal up, because he had conducted the surveillance himself. It was four nights ago at a trendy singles bar in downtown Auckland.

He relaxed marginally as Eva detached Kendal's arm with the kind of brisk efficiency that spelled out loud and clear that whatever bargain she had struck with Kendal, it was purely business. Which suited Kyle, since Kendal had the kind of reputation with women that sent a cold itch down his spine.

Kyle found a seat in the shadow of a large indoor palm, where he could keep an eye on Eva and Troy. Taking out his phone, he made a call to a contact. His family's bank poured a lot of money into sponsoring professional rugby. A few minutes later, after pledging a further personal donation from his own funds, contingent on a contract offer to Kendal, he hung up.

A waiter placed a plate of food in front of him. Kyle ate without tasting, intent on Kendal as the man took a call on his cell. Minutes later, Kendal left the wedding with a pretty blonde who had been seated at his table.

Kyle's phone buzzed. After receiving confirmation that Kendal had verbally accepted a contract offer, he terminated the call and sat back in his chair.

Eva wouldn't be happy with him. She was smart and would know exactly what he had done, but Kyle couldn't regret getting rid of Kendal. He was the kind of unsavory guy he wouldn't trust with any of the women he knew, family or not.

With Kendal now out of the picture, Eva's last marriage scheme had just collapsed.

The thought filled him with relief. If Eva had picked someone she could love, he would not have intervened. Instead, she had chosen a list of controllable men who really did just want money. Losers who were not immune to the fact that Eva was drop-dead gorgeous and distractingly sexy. Kyle knew exactly how the masculine mind worked. Platonic agreement or not, it would have only been a matter of time before Eva would have found herself maneuvered into bed.

His stomach tightened on a hot punch of emotion.

Over his dead body.

Kendal sliding his arm around Eva's waist had sealed his decision in stone.

Eva had turned him down, but in the space of an hour the game had changed. She wanted him. Up until now he had been content to keep his distance and let Eva exhaust her options, but now he was no longer prepared to stand back or let any other man enter the picture. She would accept his proposal; it was just a matter of time.

Eva was his.

Four

Eva shoveled a chunk of the gorgeous wedding cake onto a plate and for good measure snagged two of the ridiculously cute frosted cupcakes and a flute of champagne. It was an undisciplined decision and the calories would go straight to her hips, but it had been hours since she had eaten. Besides, since it was supposed to be her wedding, she figured she deserved a little comfort food.

Irritated with the glasses, which were pressing hard enough on the bridge of her nose to give her a headache, she dragged them off and tucked them in her pocket. The music was still pounding in the main reception room, but the bride and groom had departed, so there was no longer any need to look nerdish. Plate in one hand, glass in the other, she scanned the room for Kyle so she could avoid him. Although, since she had acknowledged the crazy, self-destructive fatal attraction that gripped her, she seemed to have developed an ultrasensitive inner radar so that, without looking, she knew exactly where he was.

When she couldn't find him, instead of being relieved, her stomach plummeted. Taller than most of the guests, he was normally easy to spot.

A wild suspicion formed that maybe he was with Jacinta, whom she had seen chatting to him on a number of occasions. The suspicion was allayed when she glimpsed Jacinta in animated conversation with the best man, who was considerably better looking than the groom.

She strolled down into the tropical gardens, where a few guests were sitting at tables, enjoying the balmy evening. The exotic plantings looked spectacular when lit at night. Kyle was nowhere to be seen, which meant he had probably left. Jaw firming against the impossible notion that the weird, plunging feeling in her stomach was disappointment, she belatedly remembered Troy.

The last time she had seen him he had been sitting with some blonde and drinking too much. Suspicious, because he had a definite reputation when it came to women, especially blonde women, she checked the dance floor. When she didn't see him there, she made a search of the hotel lobby and loitered near the men's room while she polished off the wedding cake and sipped a little more champagne. When Troy didn't appear, she strolled to the pool area.

The patio, which was fringed with palms and drifts of star jasmine that scented the night, was dimly lit and lonely. The enormous pool was empty of bathers, its surface limpid, the lights under the water giving it a jewel-like glow. Eva checked the bathing pavilion, which held changing rooms, showers and stacks of fluffy white towels. It, too, was empty. With the way her luck was running lately, she had to consider that either Troy had left with the blonde, or they had gotten a room together.

She should have been disappointed, but the plain fact was she had not liked Troy. Sitting down on a deck chair, she finished off the last of the champagne. Instead of leaving the flute on the pavers, where it could be knocked over and shattered, she decided to store it in her bag until she could drop it back at the bar.

She stared gloomily at the cupcakes. She was halfway through the chocolate one with fudge icing and pretty sugar flowers when a deep, curt voice cut through even that meager pleasure. "If you were looking for Kendal, he left."

"With the blonde?"

"With the blonde."

Eva slapped what was left of the cupcake back on the plate and tried to ignore the dizzying relief that while Troy had left, Kyle was still here. It was an odd time to note that while every man she had handpicked and tried to organize into her life—for just a brief time, and for money— had run out on her, the one man she had been desperate to avoid and who didn't need money, had stayed. "What did you say to him?"

Kyle emerged from the shadows of the palms, where she knew there was a shell path that led to the beach. Her stomach tensed. It was a path she could hardly forget, since it was the one she and Kyle had taken years ago when they had sneaked away to share their one and only passionate interlude. The awareness that was becoming more and more acute hummed through her like an electric current. A little desperately, she picked up the lemon cupcake with white chocolate icing and a delicate sprinkling of raspberry dust, although her appetite was gone.

Kyle dropped his jacket, which he'd slung over one

shoulder, over the back of a deck chair and walked around the pool toward her. "I didn't say a word to Kendal."

She tried not to be mesmerized by the way the pool lights glanced off the taut lines of his cheekbones and jaw, investing his skin with a bronze sheen as if he really was a warrior of old. "You've gotten rid of every other man, so why not Troy?"

He undid a couple of buttons and loosened off his tie, unwittingly drawing her gaze to the muscular column of his throat. Swallowing, she looked away from that fascinating triangle of tanned skin and ended up studying a scar that made a small, intriguing crescent on one cheekbone. For the first time she noticed that he had dark circles beneath his eyes, as if he hadn't been getting enough sleep.

Join the club, she thought, firmly squashing any hint of compassion. Just because an old attraction that should have died years ago had somehow reactivated, that didn't mean her brain had turned to mush. If Kyle had let her marry any one of the grooms she had chosen, they would both be getting plenty of sleep.

He paused just feet away. "Kendal's agent made him an offer he couldn't refuse."

There was a moment of weird disorientation, where ordinary sounds and sensations seemed to blink out, and yet her heart pumped so loudly it was deafening. She looked down and saw the lemon cupcake had turned to mangled chunks between her fingers. Dropping the remains of the cupcake on the plate, she grabbed the napkin that was folded to one side of the plate and wiped icing off her fingers.

Losing her temper wouldn't get her anywhere with Kyle. As long as she could remember, he had been utterly male, as blunt and immovable as a rock wall. Crazily, that was what had once attracted her so much. When her teenage world had been in pieces, he had seemed strong and disciplined in a quiet, steady way. Special forces had suited him down to the ground. "Money. I should have guessed."

He strolled to the edge of the pool. "Kendal's got a reputation. You wouldn't have been able to handle him."

"So you decided to handle him for me." She launched to her feet, too upset to stay. But in her hurry, she forgot that she had dropped her bag by the recliner, and in the dim light she didn't see the strap lying on the pavers. One of her heels snagged in the strap and she stumbled.

Strong fingers closed around her upper arm, steadying her. Her reaction was instantaneous as she jerked free and shoved at Kyle's chest. She had a split second to register how near she was to the edge of the pool. Kyle said something curt and grabbed at her wrist, but it was too late as the glossy surface of the water came up to meet her.

The cool water was a shock, but not as much as Kyle, whom she must have pulled off balance, plunging into the water beside her. Holding her breath, she kicked to the surface and tried to ignore the fact that she had left her shoes at the bottom of the pool. Pale pink to match her suit, and superexpensive, she had loved them with passion, but no way was she diving back in to get them with Kyle watching. She would wait until he was gone then fish them out later.

Swimming to the ladder, she climbed out, trying not to be aware of Kyle boosting himself over the side in one lithe movement. She was still angry with him, but it was difficult to sustain fury when her clothes were wet and clinging, her hair had collapsed into a bedraggled mess and every time she looked at Kyle, his wet shirt plastered to his chest, her mind went utterly blank.

Kyle dragged off his tie and peeled out of his shirt. Averting her gaze from his impressive torso, Eva walked briskly into the poolroom and retrieved two towels from the nearest shelf. Tossing one at Kyle, she kept her eyes averted as she dried herself off.

Instead of using the towel, Kyle draped it over a nearby lounger and dropped back down into the pool. Seconds later, he climbed back out with her shoes. Water slid off bronzed skin and dripped from his nose as he handed them to her. "I'm sorry I pushed you so hard."

Eva ruthlessly suppressed the desire to respond to the glimpse of humor since, technically, she was the one who had done the pushing. Grimly, she concentrated on drying the shoes. She absolutely did not want to start remembering all the moments they had shared all those years ago and start thinking of him as funny or sweet. They'd had their moment, and it hadn't worked out. "I'm glad I pushed you. You deserved it."

The quick flash of a grin almost stopped her heart. "Still the same old Eva."

And who, exactly, was that? she wondered a little bitterly. Years ago she had come to the conclusion that he saw her as a messed-up adopted kid. The kind of woman no Messena male in his right mind would date, let alone marry.

To cover up the fact that she was having difficulty keeping her gaze off his torso and a smattering of scars that looked suspiciously like knife or maybe even bullet wounds, she gripped the back of a lounger to put on first one shoe, then the other. She knew Kyle had been injured twice, the second time life threatening enough that he'd been medevaced from Germany back to Auckland.

That time, she had been concerned enough that she had rung the hospital to get an update on his condition.

When they had refused to do that over the phone, she had
gone there herself, brazening her way onto Kyle's ward,
even though visiting hours had finished. When she had
finally found him, she had used her family connection
to the Messenas and her celebrity status as a model to
get into his room.

She had been shocked to see him pale and still and
hooked up to monitors and drips, then a senior nurse had
walked in and she'd had to leave. That had been just as
well, because as she'd walked out the door Kyle's eyes
had flickered open.

Dragging pins from her soaked hair and finger combing it out into some semblance of neatness, she couldn't
resist the compulsion to sneak another glance at the worst
of the scars and, inadvertently, found herself caught out
by Kyle's gaze.

"I know that was you, all those years ago at the hospital."

She froze. "Maybe."

He raked wet hair back from his forehead. "I thought
I was dreaming, but the nurse confirmed it."

She busied herself picking up her bag in order to drop
the pins into it, but she wasn't paying close enough attention, so some of them scattered over the pavers. Crouching down, she began gathering them up. "It was no big
deal. I was in town and heard you'd been—hurt—"

"As in, wounded." He handed her a pin that had skit-
tered over by his foot.

She straightened and found herself uncomfortably
close to his naked and still-damp torso. "I didn't want to
say that, just in case you had that condition—"

"Post-traumatic stress disorder. Battle fatigue." His
mouth quirked in a distractingly sexy way. "No chance,

since I have no memory of being hit." He hesitated. "Why didn't you stay?"

Eva, still captured by the sudden intense need to know what exactly had happened, *who* had dared to shoot Kyle, took a few seconds to absorb his question. "You were critical—they wouldn't let me stay."

"I was only critical the night I arrived. I didn't see any family until the next day. So, how did you find out?"

Despite her clothes, which were steadily dripping, and which were now making her feel clammy and just a little chilled, she found herself blushing. There was no way she was going to tell Kyle that she had practically lived on the internet, tracking down Reuters reports, and that she had made a pest of herself by calling his regimental headquarters. "I had a modeling friend whose boyfriend was in the SAS." That part was true enough. She shrugged. "I just happened to mention that you'd been hurt and she…found out for me."

"But you didn't visit me again."

She straightened, hooking the strap of her bag over her shoulder. "I was *busy*. What is this? An interrogation?" Although something about Kyle had changed. The bad-tempered tension had gone and there was an undercurrent that made her feel decidedly breathless. She tried walking in her wet heels to see if they were safe. At the same time she surreptitiously smoothed her palms down the sodden, clinging line of her jacket and skirt to press out excess moisture. As a result, water tickled down her legs and filled her shoes.

Kyle stopped in the process of wringing out his shirt, his gaze arrested. "Maybe you should take the jacket off?"

"No." Eva had routinely taken her clothes off for lingerie ads, but there was no way she was going to take one stitch of clothing off in front of Kyle. She suddenly noticed the flatness of her jacket pocket. Her glasses were gone, which meant they were probably in the bottom of the pool.

"They can stay there," Kyle said flatly. "You don't need them. You've got the eyesight of an eagle."

"How would you know what my eyesight's like?"

"Remember the archery contests?"

Dolphin Bay, two summers in a row, when she and Kyle would go head-to-head at the archery range. "You always won those."

"I'd been practicing for years. You came second."

The sudden warmth in his gaze made her feel flustered all over again. She realized that the distance she had worked so hard to preserve, and which she had been able to maintain quite well if she was angry, had gone. Burned away in the moment she had realized that Kyle wanted her.

She walked to the edge of the pool and peered in. The glasses, with their dark rims, were easily visible. "I need the glasses for work."

"Why? They're not prescription, just plain glass." His face cleared. "No, wait, don't answer, I think I can guess."

Over seeing Kyle's buff, ripped, *hot* torso, she tossed his towel at him. A split second later the sharp tap of heels on tiles signaled Jacinta's presence a moment before she rounded the corner into the pool area.

Her eyes widened when she saw that Eva was soaked. "There you are, the bride's father wants to give you a check—" She noticed Kyle. "Oops. Sorry, did I interrupt something?"

"Nothing." Eva seized her chance to end the unsettling encounter and the crazy, suffocating awareness that had crept up on her out of nowhere. "Where is Mr. Hirsch?"

"In the lobby." Jacinta glanced at Kyle's washboard abs. "I told him you'd be right along."

But suddenly, Eva wasn't going anywhere. She took the one step needed to place herself squarely in Jacinta's line of vision, so that she had to stare at her, rather than at Kyle's bronzed, dripping skin. In the moment that she moved, it struck her that she was behaving like a jealous girlfriend. Kyle did not belong to her, and yet she was ready to fight tooth and nail to fend Jacinta off. "I'm wet and my hair's ruined. You need to go and collect the check."

Jacinta didn't move. "Did you fall in the pool?"

"We both fell," Eva said bluntly.

Jacinta made an odd little noise that sounded suspiciously like amusement quickly muffled then spun on her heel and disappeared back inside.

Kyle broke the tense little silence that developed in the wake of Jacinta's departure by tossing his towel on a recliner and picking up his soaked shirt. "At least you managed to sell the wedding on. I'm guessing right about now, you're getting concerned about money."

She met Kyle's gaze head-on. "Without the backup of my trust fund, all money counts."

And that was the other reason she found this whole process of having to qualify for her own inheritance so hurtful and undermining. All of the bona fide Atraeus and Messena family members who were born to wealth received vast amounts of money, and their right to do so wasn't questioned. She understood what Mario was trying to achieve with the marriage clause, but that didn't change the fact that the whole process made her feel separated from the rest of the family, and *different*.

Stung anew by what she saw as further evidence that, despite adoption, she had never quite fitted into the Atraeus family, Eva turned on her heel, intending to make a beeline for her car, where she had a pair of jeans, a T-shirt and sneakers stashed for the drive back to Auckland.

Kyle caught her arm, halting her. "I'm sorry. I shouldn't have mentioned the money."

The tingling warmth of Kyle's palm, even through the barrier of damp silk, sent a small, sharp shock through her. She jerked free. "I suppose you think I'm a money-grubbing gold digger who doesn't deserve—"

"I don't think that." His gaze dropped to her mouth. "You deserve your inheritance."

Her chin jerked up. "Then why have you been doing your level best to deprive me of it?"

"Money isn't the issue," he muttered. "This is." Bending his head, Kyle kissed her.

Eva inhaled sharply at the warmth of his mouth, stunned by the brief caress and the molten heat that exploded from that one point of contact. When she didn't move, Kyle's palm curled around her nape. The next minute she was pressed hard against the muscled heat of his body as his mouth settled more heavily on hers.

The passion was searing and instant and this time, Eva wasn't content to just be kissed. Palms flattened against the hard muscle of Kyle's chest, and all too aware that she was making a disastrous mistake, she lifted up on her toes and angled her head to increase the contact. His taste exploded in her mouth and the furnace heat of his body warmed her, so that she wanted to press closer still, to wallow in his heat and strength.

And suddenly, it registered just how alone and isolated she had been. Since her teenage fixation on Kyle, she had simply not allowed anyone else close. She had sidestepped relationships and sex. She hadn't thought she needed either, until now.

The strap of her bag slipped off her shoulder. She registered the thump as it dropped onto the ground, and the sound of glass breaking and dimly remembered the champagne flute. Her arms closed around Kyle's neck as the kiss deepened, and suddenly the cling of her wet clothes seemed sodden and restrictive, dragging against skin that was unbearably sensitive. His hand cupped her breast through the layers of wet fabric. Eva inhaled at the sharp beading of her nipple, but it was too late as heat and sensation coiled unbearably tight and splintered.

Kyle muttered something short beneath his breath. Eva pulled free of his grasp, her legs as limp as noodles, embarrassed warmth burning through her. Not only had she practically thrown herself at Kyle like some love-starved teenager, she had actually climaxed just because he had kissed her.

Dragging damp tendrils back from her face, she snatched up her bag and noticed that the champagne flute had broken at the stem and was in two pieces. Jaw set, she found the cake napkin and wrapped the base of the flute.

Kyle crouched down beside her and handed her the rest of the flute but, with her whole body still oversensitive and tingling, Kyle helping, Kyle intruding any further into her life was the last thing she wanted.

"Eva—"

She straightened, desperate to avoid him, but he rose lithely and blocked her path.

Too late to wish that she'd searched for her compact and checked her makeup. Her mascara was probably running. She must look a total mess—

"You wanted to know why I vetoed the grooms you chose. Two reasons. None of them were good enough. And I couldn't let you marry anyone else because *I* want you."

Five

Eva stared at Kyle.

I want you.

A small, sensual shiver zapped down her spine. Not good! She should be annoyed at the way Kyle had gotten rid of all the men she had chosen, not turned on and reveling in the fact that he had done so because he thought none of them had been good enough. "Let me get this right. You proposed because you want sex?"

Suddenly irritated beyond belief, she rummaged in her handbag, found her cell and stabbed a random icon. "Wait just one second. I'm sure I have an app you need called Sex Slaves Are Us."

Impatience registered in his gaze. "I proposed because you need a husband."

Somehow that was the wrong answer. "So sex would just be an optional extra?"

There was a small, vibrating silence. "Whether or not sex would be part of the deal is entirely up to you."

The anger that rolled through Eva was knee-jerk and confusing. She had been angry that Kyle wanted sex from her. Now she was even angrier because, evidently, he could take it or leave it. In her book, that brought them back to square one. She just wasn't that important to Kyle. And didn't that just feel like a replay of the past?

She jammed her cell back in her bag. Until that moment she hadn't realized how much Kyle's defection all those years ago still hurt. He had been a friend when she had needed one. She hadn't just wanted him at age seventeen; she had liked and trusted him. He had walked away without a backward glance then fallen in love with *and married* someone else.

She should have let this go a long time ago. It was neither healthy, nor balanced. But then, balance had never been her strong point. She had always been passionate and a little extreme. Of course, letting go of the hurt of Kyle's rejection was difficult, because in her heart of hearts she had felt sure that they had been on the verge of something special.

On the heels of that thought, suspicion flared. "Did Mario suggest you should marry me before he died?"

Kyle's gaze turned wary. "He did."

Now she really was embarrassed. Mario had been convinced that, despite her disorder, as an heiress she could have the same kind of happy married life he'd had with his wife, if she would only follow the old recipe and marry someone wealthy, trusted and close to home. He had relentlessly tried to marry her off in that way to Kyle's older brothers and, to her everlasting relief, he hadn't succeeded in raising even a flicker of interest. "I know for a fact that he asked Gabriel and Nick and they both turned him down."

Kyle shrugged. "That was a given, since they were both in love with other women."

Eva swiped at a renegade trickle of water sliding down her neck, suddenly incensed. "And who would buy into that crazy kind of medieval stuff, anyway?"

Kyle dragged his gaze from the creamy line of Eva's neck and the tantalizing hint of cleavage in the vee of her suit jacket.

He would.

Although, obviously, that did not reflect well on him. "If you're so set on a marriage of convenience, then I don't get why you're so against taking the second option in the will."

"And marry you?" Eva's chin came up. "Because, while Messena and Atraeus men may look and sound like modern twenty-first century guys, they aren't. Underneath that veneer every one of you is just as medieval as Mario was. And I don't want children. Ever."

The flat certainty of Eva's statement hit Kyle in the solar plexus.

Children. He had a sudden mental image of his small son, Evan, who had been just three months old when he had died.

His stomach tightened on the kind of grief no parent should ever feel as memory flickered. Evan, soft and warm on his shoulder, well fed and smelling of soap and milk as he had relaxed into sleep. The way he had used to crow with delight every time Kyle had picked him up...

When he spoke, he couldn't keep the grim chill out of his voice. "Children won't be an issue, because I don't want them, either. But in any case, we're only looking at an arrangement that will last two years."

He logged the flare of shock in her gaze. He had been

too abrasive. But when it came to the issue of marriage and kids, he couldn't be any other way.

His own family didn't understand him. But then, none of them had seen his wife and child disappear in an explosion that had killed five others and destroyed the barracks gatehouse. None of them understood that moment of sickening displacement, the knowledge that Nicola and Evan would be alive now if it wasn't for *his* insistence that they join him in Germany for Christmas.

The shock of their deaths and the weight of grief and guilt still had the power to stop him in his tracks. It was the reason he avoided friends who had kids and family occasions that, increasingly, overflowed with babies and small children. It was the reason he steered clear of anything approaching a conventional relationship, because he knew he couldn't be that person again. Just the thought of taking on the responsibility of a wife and child made him break out in a cold sweat. His oldest brother, Gabriel, who had arrived in Germany just hours after the explosion, was the only one who had an inkling about how he felt. He unlocked his jaw and tried to soften his tone. "If you agree to marriage, you set the terms."

She crossed her arms over her chest, her stance combative. "Let me see, everything but children, and you would prefer sex as an additional extra."

His gaze narrowed at the way she phrased the same kind of straightforward marriage deal she had personally negotiated at least three times in the past six months. Except for the sex. And he couldn't help a savage little jolt of satisfaction at that fact. "Yes."

She took a half step toward him. He registered the fiery glint in her eyes as she came to a halt in front of him and trailed her finger from a point just below his collarbone to the midpoint of his chest.

"Marriage to you? Now, let me see…" Her gaze locked with his, and he knew very well that she didn't intend to kiss him. "That would be a clear…*no*."

And with a shove she sent him toppling back into the pool.

The following night Eva prepared to go to a trendy singles bar with a couple of girlfriends. She hated singles bars and normally would never go to one but, after the debacle with Kyle, she was determined to make one more attempt at locating a husband.

Kyle's proposal was an unexpected goad. The fact that she personally wanted him had somehow made the situation even more fraught. Her response to his kiss had been a case in point. She'd never been able to resist him, and now he knew it. If they married, even if she said no to sex, would she be strong enough to hold out against him?

She flipped through her wardrobe for something to wear. She needed something that was sexy but reserved enough that she could attract a man who was reasonably good-looking, intelligent and down on his luck. She doubted she would find the type of man she needed at a singles bar, since most men who went there just wanted sex, but she had to try.

She chose a little black dress and pumps that weren't too high, because she was already medium height and she didn't want to narrow her options by being too tall. After putting on makeup, she combed her hair out straight so that it swung silkily around her shoulders. Affixing tawny earrings to her lobes, she spritzed herself with perfume and she was good to go.

The bar was packed. After ordering a drink, she sat at a cozy sofa and coffee table setting. Feeling like a wallflower, Eva sipped the iced water she had ordered.

Seconds later, she had her first approach, a handsome dark-haired guy who looked like a lawyer and proved to be. She sent him on his way when she found out he was married.

Two more conversations later with men who up front admitted they were married, but had left their wives—which meant they were utterly useless to her because they couldn't remarry until they were legally divorced—she scanned the bar. Depressingly, most of the men at the bar were either already hooked up with a partner or looked older, which from experience she knew probably meant they would still be married, even if they weren't living with their wives.

She caught a glimpse of the back of a guy's head as he disappeared into a shadowy part of the bar. Adrenaline pumped, because she was certain it was Kyle. He was the right height and his shoulders were broad. He half turned, giving her a clear view of his profile. It wasn't Kyle.

Unacceptably, disappointment deflated her mood even further. Of course none of the Messena men would be seen dead in a singles bar. They were too wealthy, too macho and too gorgeous. They didn't need to go after women, because women chased them. Jacinta's reaction to Kyle was a case in point. She had practically swooned over him.

A nerdy guy approached her and asked if she would like to dance. Eva checked out his left hand and saw the pale streak around his third finger. "Why don't you ask your wife to dance?"

"Uh—she's out of town."

"And I thought this was a *singles* bar. You should go home."

His face reddened. "Who are you? My grandmother?"

She gave him a straight look. "If I was, I'd be saying a whole lot more."

After biting out an uncomplimentary phrase, he spun on his heel and strode away. All pleasure was now leeched from the evening. In no mood to date, or marry, anyone, Eva pulled out her phone and checked an app that listed nearby nightclubs and bars.

She didn't want to go anywhere else. She would prefer to go home, make a cup of tea, curl up on the sofa and watch a movie, but she couldn't give up just yet.

She stepped outside of the air-conditioned bar into the hot, steamy air of a summer's night. It was like walking into a sauna. Glancing skyward, she noticed the heavy layer of cloud that had rolled in, blotting out the night sky. Because Auckland City was situated on a narrow isthmus with the Tasman Sea on one side, the Pacific Ocean on the other, the weather could change quickly.

Hailing a cab, she gave the driver the address of a bar she'd used before that was younger and a little wilder. She'd met Troy there, and that would have worked out if it hadn't been for Kyle.

He had vetoed every other guy she had chosen, and she couldn't help thinking that if she located a possible groom tonight, he would no doubt suffer the same fate.

Kyle wanted her.

She tried to dismiss the disruptive thought, but heat flooded her at the memory of the kiss and the way she had reacted, like a love-starved teenager on her first date! She breathed a sigh of relief as the driver pulled away from the curb and the cab's air-conditioning kicked in. Something made her glance back at the entrance of the bar. A tall, dark-haired man was just sliding behind the wheel of a glossy black sports car. Her heart slammed in her chest at the thought that it was Kyle, although she couldn't be sure. There were a lot of dark sports cars in town, which all looked the same to her, and maybe she was seeing the same guy she had noticed before?

If it was Kyle, that meant he was following her. A sharp thrill jolted through her at the thought.

Determinedly, she squashed the idea along with any hint of relief that despite her saying no, Kyle might not have given up on her. Keeping her gaze fixed on the city street ahead, she tried to remember all the reasons she had to be furious with him. Unfortunately, the reasons seemed hollow when she kept coming back to the stunning fact that he had actually asked her to marry him.

And she was wondering if the offer was still open.

Craning around, she looked through the back window. The car was following so closely it was practically herding the taxi, but the windows of the sleek sports car were too darkly tinted to reveal who was driving. The driver could see her, but she couldn't see him. Her heart pounded out of control. She was suddenly certain that it was Kyle.

The taxi pulled into a space and the sports car swept past. Eva paid the fare and climbed out, all the while giving herself a good talking-to. She should be frustrated and annoyed if it was Kyle—she should be furious—so why did it feel like the evening was suddenly looking up?

In the time it took her to close the door of the taxi, the sports car had disappeared. She checked in both directions, half expecting to see Kyle walking toward her. When she realized she was loitering on the sidewalk, actually waiting for him to appear, instead of going into the bar closest to where the taxi had parked, she quickly walked a little further down the road before spotting another random bar.

Pulse rate still high, she checked the street one last

time before walking in, only to find she had another problem. Now that she was here, she had absolutely no energy or enthusiasm for finding a suitable husband. Her experience at the previous bar had literally been the last straw.

Kyle was right. She did not want a stranger for a husband.

She could still say yes to Kyle. But if she allowed the attraction that sizzled through her every time she saw Kyle to turn into actual love, where would that leave her in two years' time?

The bar she'd chosen was an Irish pub, filled with young people and a sprinkling of tourists. Feeling too put-together and conventional amongst skin-tight denim, shaved heads and psychedelic tattoos, she took a stool at the counter, dropped her chin on one hand and ordered a glass of wine.

The bartender, who looked ridiculously young and was probably a student, instantly started chatting her up. "Don't I know you from somewhere?"

Eva sipped her drink and logged the moment he recognized her.

He nodded his head, grinning. "Oh yeah. The buses. The lingerie ad."

She groaned inwardly, but managed to keep her expression bland. She'd had a lot of practice handling these kinds of conversations, since the lingerie company she had worked for had plastered images of her on the back of buses and on huge highway billboards. "That was a while ago." Two years. Although it felt like ten.

"Cool. My mom used to buy your stuff."

Eva set her glass down and checked her watch. She had promised herself she would stay for fifteen minutes. By then, Kyle should have found a parking space and gone inside the other bar and she could safely leave without him seeing her. "I didn't own the company, I just modeled for them."

He grinned again. "Still…nice. Those billboards were *big*. Most of the buses in town had you on the back of them. Pretty sure some of them still do." He leaned forward on the bar, angling for a better view down the front of her dress. "If you're still into that kind of work, I've got a friend—"

"She doesn't do charities for school kids."

The rasp of Kyle's voice sent a hot tingle down her spine as he slid onto a stool beside her. Dressed all in black, a five-o'clock shadow darkening his jaw, his gaze wintry, he looked, quite frankly, intimidating.

Eva felt like banging her head on the counter. Former Special Air Service, an assault specialist who had once belonged to some hunter-killer squad with its own scary code name… Why, oh why, had she not known he would find her?

His gaze touched on hers and her fingers tightened convulsively on the stem of her wineglass. Taking a deep breath because her heart was suddenly racing, she dredged up a dazzling smile for the bartender who, predictably, was backing off fast. "Actually, I *would* like to speak to your friend. As it happens, in about three weeks' time I'll be in the market for some modeling work."

"Uh—my friend's more into *movies*, you know? Maybe, talk to me later." His gaze flickered to Kyle, the subtext clear. *When the boyfriend's gone.*

"He's not my boyfriend."

A nervous tic jumped along one side of the bartender's jaw. He glanced around, as if willing a customer to appear. "On second thoughts, I seem to remember my friend's getting ready to go overseas…"

And if she didn't miss her guess, the bartender was getting ready to run.

Drawn by a compulsion she couldn't seem to resist, she met Kyle's gaze and tried not to notice the instant little charge of adrenaline that shot through her at the laser blue of his eyes. Trying to ignore the tension thrumming through her, she ran her finger around the rim of the wineglass. "Do you have to ruin everything? Lately, I feel like I live in some kind of Mafia family."

"If you want modeling work, there are better places to get it than over the bar of some pub, like your agent, for instance."

"What would you know about it?"

"The bank has modeling agencies as clients. I don't know how they run their businesses, but I'm pretty sure it's not at—" he looked at the sign over the bar "—Irish Jack's."

She sent him a sideways glance that was supposed to be withering, then wished she hadn't when she caught the gleam of humor in his eyes. She squashed the sudden, almost irresistible desire to smile with him. "My agent still has clients lining up. I can continue my modeling career if I want."

"In movies?"

"I don't do movies. I just said that to annoy you."

"You succeeded."

Feeling a little panicky, because she did not want to love Kyle's dry sense of humor or the possessiveness, she slipped off the barstool. Maybe if she were standing, she would feel more in control. Unfortunately, Kyle also stood, towering over her, making her feel ridiculously small and feminine.

She made a beeline for the door but couldn't suppress her automatic pleasure at the small courtesy when Kyle held it for her. In her current state of mind, she could not afford to be charmed by Kyle's manners.

When she stepped out into the balmy evening air, she spun and confronted him. "Is the offer of marriage still open?" The words tumbled out sounding a whole lot more vulnerable than she'd planned.

His gaze sharpened. "Why? What's changed?"

She swallowed at the leap he'd made, his scary insight. Because something had changed. She'd felt it in the instant he had sat down at the bar and fended off the bartender. She didn't know exactly what had changed, just that she had *liked* it that Kyle wanted to protect her. "I'm not sure. I'm confused."

"The offer is still open." He was silent for a moment. "If you want, I can give you a lift home."

She frowned at the sudden switch from aggressive pursuit to coolness. The sense of hidden depth and layers abruptly made her aware of the abyss that lay between the teenaged Kyle she had once fallen for, and the mature, seasoned man who stood in front of her now. "Okay."

The lights of Kyle's Maserati, which occupied a parking spot further along the road, flashed. A short walk later, he opened the passenger side door for her. Taking a deep breath, careful not to brush against him, she settled into the luxurious seat, stomach clenching at the subtly masculine scent of leather. The door closed and seconds later, Kyle slid behind the wheel and the car accelerated off the curb.

As they cruised through town, stopping at intersections filled with tourists enjoying the restaurants and cafés, and loved-up couples strolling, she suddenly didn't want the night to end. "I don't want to go home. Not yet."

He turned his head, and she caught the glitter of

his gaze. The tension in the enclosed space seemed to tighten. "Where do you want to go?"

"The beach." The answer came straight out of the past and made warmth rise to her cheeks, because she belatedly realized the link to their long-ago tryst. It was just that the beach had been such a carefree place for her. She'd spent long summers at Dolphin Bay swimming and sunbathing and building late-night fires. Adoptive cousins, most like Kyle—second and third times removed— and extended family everywhere, and her old life with its trouble and grief left far behind.

Kyle took a turn in the direction of the marina. Traffic slowed. Ahead, Eva glimpsed a bus and hoped it wasn't one of the ones that still had the underwear ad. And, of course, it was.

Kyle sent her a neutral look. "That's one of the reasons Mario worried about you."

Eva studied the faintly battered line of Kyle's profile, the tough jaw and ridiculously long, silky lashes. She shrugged. She wasn't about to apologize for a highly successful modeling career. "Mario was conservative."

She switched her gaze to his hands on the wheel. A scar started at the sleeve of his shirt and ran the length of the back of his hand. "How did you get that?"

He frowned. "Don't change the subject."

"You always want to talk about me. Maybe I want to talk about you."

The minute the words were out, she wished she hadn't said them, because they sounded flirtatious and provocative.

"It's a fishing injury from a couple of years ago. Nick was casting and his hook caught me."

"I thought it might be from the military."

Amusement flashed in his gaze. "Disappointed?"

"No! That last injury putting you in the hospital was bad enough. You almost died." Her stomach bottomed out at the thought. It was almost four years ago, but she could still remember how frantic she'd felt. She hadn't questioned her reaction then, she had just thought it was a leftover of the crush she'd had on Kyle. But how long did crushes last?

Kyle changed lanes and accelerated smoothly. "When I woke up, Gabriel told me that if I didn't resign, he would join up. I knew he'd keep his word, and that the family and the bank couldn't afford to lose him, so I signed the discharge papers."

"You didn't want to leave? I don't know how you could have wanted to stay in after—"

"Nicola and Evan were killed?"

She stared ahead, the stream of oncoming traffic a colorful blur. "I'm sorry, I shouldn't have mentioned it. I know what it's like losing people you love. It's hard to believe they're gone."

She registered his curious gaze, as if he were waiting for her to elaborate. But she'd said too much already. She'd found that the less she said about her past, the better she fitted in. Ignoring the past didn't make it go away, but it sure helped her to feel more normal.

Kyle took an off-ramp and stopped for lights. "It was an attack on the barracks where we were based in Germany," he said quietly. "Unfortunately, Nicola was driving past the car with the explosives when it detonated. Evan was in his car seat. It was pure bad luck. If she had been a few seconds earlier or later, they would have avoided the blast."

There was a moment of silence. "If I hadn't insisted they come out to Germany for Christmas, they would still be alive."

The words, uttered flatly, nevertheless contained a rawness that riveted Eva. She didn't know why she hadn't considered that Kyle might blame himself for the death of his wife and child, but the flat statement made a terrible kind of sense.

Kyle was an alpha male. Testosterone aside, that meant taking charge and taking responsibility. To have lost the two people most intimately connected with him, the wife and child he had vowed to care for and protect, must be unbearable. In that instant a whole lot of things she hadn't understood about Kyle settled into place. Foremost was the fact that he had *loved* his wife and child.

A sharp ache started somewhere deep in her chest. The way she, all those years ago, would have loved to be loved. "You still miss them."

The lights changed, Kyle accelerated through the intersection. "Birthdays and important dates are the worst, but it's not as bad as it used to be."

"I'm sorry." As much as she had gotten used to loss and grief, the process of losing her family over a period of years had, at least, given her time to adjust. She could not imagine what it must have been like for Kyle to lose a wife and child, literally, in an instant.

He took the off-ramp for Takapuna Beach, his expression closed. "It's okay. It hurt, but it was years ago."

She stared ahead at the road as it unfolded, feeling suddenly incredibly self-centered. She had been viewing Kyle as controlling and intrusive—the big, bad wolf—but like all the men in his family, he was a family man.

Abruptly, she understood him in a way that was unbearably and intimately personal. As the oldest child in her family, she had said goodbye to her twin and two younger siblings. She could remember holding their hands and willing them to live. One by one they had died; there had been nothing she could do. It wasn't the shock of a bomb blast, but the sense of helplessness was the same.

Kyle turned down a side street then into a park, with the sea just a few yards from a small parking lot. Now that they were alone, and at the beach, she was out of stall time.

Panic gripped her. Given that she now knew she could not marry a stranger, she needed to decide whether or not she could cope with a temporary marriage to Kyle.

Six

Kyle tossed his jacket in the space behind the driver's seat and walked around the hood of the Maserati to open the passenger side door. Predictably, Eva already had the door open, but was still seated while she unfastened her shoes. He drew in a breath at the elegant line of her legs and the tantalizing glimmer of a fine chain around one slim ankle. "If you want to walk, I don't know how long we'll have. The forecast is for rain."

It was actually for a thunderstorm. He could already see lightning flashes farther north, and from the drop in temperature the rain could start any time.

"Don't care." She sent him a fleeting look that, half hidden by a tousled swath of tawny hair, was unconsciously sexy.

His stomach tightened as he was irresistibly reminded of a seventeen-year-old girl who had trailed endlessly along the beach at Dolphin Bay in a bikini top and a pair of ragged, cutoff denim shorts, driving most of the male population crazy.

She slid out of the Maserati, the gusting breeze plastering her little black dress against the lithe curves of her body as she closed the car with a brisk thud that made him wince.

She sent him a smooth, closed smile, the kind he'd gotten familiar with lately, as if he was one of her difficult clients. "I'm tired of the city and miles of concrete. I want to feel sand between my toes."

He depressed his key and locked the car before walking to the beach. Eva was already standing on smooth, hard-packed sand, just inches shy of the water, her expression oddly relaxed.

"I love it, especially when there's going to be a storm." She sent him a slanting sideways look as he joined her, as if she was trying to assess him in some way. She smiled encouragingly. "Shall we walk?"

His jaw tightened as he suddenly got it. After months of avoidance, Eva had changed tack completely. Every muscle in his body tightened when he realized that Eva's question outside the Irish pub about whether or not his offer of marriage was still open had been for real. And that some time between that moment and the drive to the beach, she had moved on to summing him up as a potential husband. When Eva began asking him about his work hours and his interests, he realized he was being interviewed.

In a weird way, it reminded him of when he was nineteen and had spent a whole summer getting to know Eva. In a lot of ways, the process had been the exact opposite of the usual pattern. She had started out so confident and self-contained it had been hard to get close to her at all.

One day, with the summer almost over and Kyle

pushed to his limits, he had saved her from an older guy
who had cornered her at the end of the beach. The tus-
sle had been brief, but when the tourist had beat a hasty
retreat, she had stared at him and blushed. She hadn't
said a word, just continued on as if it hadn't happened,
but from that moment on her behavior had changed. In
a weird way it was as if he had passed some kind of test.

She strolled down to the water's edge, wading in ankle-
deep. There was no attempt to look sexy or alluring, just
a simple enjoyment of the seaside. She turned, her gaze
connected with his then dropped to his mouth before she
looked quickly away.

Every muscle in his body suddenly taut, Kyle waited
her out. He wanted Eva, and she knew it. Last night he
thought he'd blown any chance of having her in his bed,
but in the space of twenty-four hours, something had
changed. Added to that, the beach setting was creating
an unsettling sense of déjà vu, as if they'd been spun
back years.

Lightning flashed, followed by a heavy roll of thunder. Simultaneously, rain pounded down.

Eva flinched at the sudden deluge, but the rain, though
torrential, wasn't cold and, besides, she loved the wild-
ness of it. Kyle jerked his head in the direction of the
car but, caught up in the adrenaline of the moment, she
grabbed his hand and pulled him toward the shelter of a
large, gnarled *pohutukawa* tree.

She sucked in a breath as they stepped beneath the
dense overhang of the tree. With the sound of the surf and
the shift of shadows as dappled light from the parking
lot flowed through the leaves, in a strange way it felt like
stepping back in time to Dolphin Bay and that first kiss.

When Kyle reeled her in close and framed her face
with his hands, the breath stopped in her lungs. She

should have extricated herself in her usual smooth, sophisticated way, but ever since Kyle had slipped onto the stool beside her in the Irish pub, she had been subtly off balance. He had been tailing her for months and had ruthlessly gotten rid of any man who had gotten too close. Now he was making no bones about the fact that *he* wanted her, and against all the odds she loved that.

And suddenly she no longer wanted to resist him. Years ago she had loved Kyle and then lost him along with the whole future she had imagined she might have as a woman, a wife and a mother. He had loved another woman, but she'd had no one. Now she had a chance at... something. If she stopped to think— But right now, with the storm pounding all around them, all she wanted to do was feel.

When she ran her palms up over his chest to his shoulders, Kyle's response was instant. Hauling her closer still, he bent his head, his breath washing over her lips. "What is it with beaches," he muttered.

Lifting up on her toes, she wrapped her arms around his neck and kissed him, the passion white-hot and instant.

Long seconds later, she wrenched her mouth free and dragged at the buttons of Kyle's shirt. He muttered something short and sharp. Dimly, she registered the loosening of the fit of her dress as the zipper tracked down, a damp blast of cool air against her skin. A split second later the dress was gone and her bra along with it.

Bending down, Kyle took one nipple in his mouth. Dizzying sensation jerked through her in waves. When he lifted his head, she remembered his shirt, but he must have shrugged out of it at some point, because she found naked skin.

Kyle groaned. "Maybe we should slow down—"

Her palms slid down over washboard abs and found the fastening of his pants. He uttered a short, soft word. Moments later, she was on her back on the sand, her dress and what she guessed was Kyle's jacket and shirt beneath her.

Kyle's fingers hooked in her panties, dragging them down. Lightning flashed, illuminating the stark planes of Kyle's face as his weight came down on her. Sucking in a sharp breath at the sheer heat of him, she wound her arms around Kyle's neck, the fierce need to keep him close momentarily blotting out coherent thought.

"Babe—there's something I need to do first." He disengaged and rolled to one side. She logged the sound of foil tearing. A condom. Thunder detonated again and the rain pattered down through the canopy of leaves, splashing on bare skin so that she shivered.

Kyle hauled her close, sheltering her with his body, and in that moment it seemed the most natural thing in the world to hook one arm around his neck and lift up for his kiss. At the same time, curious about the condom, her fingers closed around him. She felt the smooth texture, the heated satin of his skin underneath.

A split second later, he came down between her legs. She felt the heated pressure of him. There was a shivering moment of sanity, when she logged Kyle's stillness, as if, like her, he had come to the sudden sobering conclusion of exactly what they were about to do. She should say no. Kyle would stop, she knew he would, and in a crazy way that in itself was freeing.

It was a plain fact that she didn't want to relinquish him or the burning, irresistible pleasure that held her in its grip. It wasn't love. She wasn't that silly, but when set against the shadows of her past and her present loneliness—the growing fear that she would never truly be cherished—it tipped an internal balance so that she no longer wanted to think, only to feel...

She felt him tense at the tight constriction and freeze in place. She thought he was going to stop, but when he lifted his head, she clung, unable to bear letting him go, arching against the burning pressure at the center of her body.

He groaned and a second later, shoved deep. She felt the drag of the condom, an uncomfortable pinching as with each downward stroke he seemed to push a little deeper still. Her hips twisted automatically, trying to ease the discomfort, but the restless twisting momentarily dislodged him.

He cradled her closer and the next downward stroke felt smoother, sleeker, more pleasurable, and she realized that something had changed. The condom was gone, but it was already too late as irresistible sensation gripped her, coiling tight, and the damp, heavy darkness shimmered into light.

Kyle stopped the car outside Eva's house. "We need to talk. Somehow, I don't know how, because it's never happened before, but the condom slipped—"

"You don't have to worry about contraception."

The words were out before she could call them back, but she couldn't regret them. She knew Kyle would probably think she was on the pill or had some other form of contraception, but that wasn't the case. She could get pregnant.

The thought made her heart beat wildly. It was the last thing she wanted, but maybe, just maybe, she could get lucky and it wouldn't happen. If it did... She drew a swift breath, unable to imagine a scenario that was so far out of left field for her.

Fingers fumbling in her haste, she unfastened her seat belt. She still felt damp, gritty and disoriented that the night had spun so far out of control that they'd actually had sex and, in the end, because the condom had come off, unprotected sex. She couldn't wait to say goodbye and escape into the quiet refuge of her home. "Thanks," she said brightly, throwing the car door open.

It was still raining. No problem, since she was already bedraggled and her dress was most likely ruined. Cheeks burning, she searched for her clutch, which had somehow managed to slide down the side of the seat. By the time she had retrieved it, Kyle was out of the car and it was too late to make a quick getaway.

Rain was cold on her bare arms as she jogged to her front door and searched for her key. Intensely aware of Kyle beside her, she jammed the key in the lock and somehow missed.

Kyle calmly took the key from her and unlocked the door. As he pushed it wide, the tinkle of glass made her freeze in place.

"Wait here," he said softly. Kyle stepped past her, flowing into the darkened interior.

A chill went down her spine at the quiet way he'd moved, his utter assurance, and despite her dilemma over whether or not to just give in and marry him, she was abruptly glad he was with her. Burglaries were common, but this was the first time it had happened to her.

Long minutes later, lights went on and Kyle reappeared in her tiny hallway. "I'll call the police. Whoever it was, they're gone now, out through the laundry door and over the back fence. The sound of breaking glass was a vase. They knocked it over on their way out."

Eva followed Kyle into her lounge. Drawers had been pulled out and emptied onto the floor. Her one framed family photo of her mother and father in happier days was sitting on the dining table, as if whoever had broken in had paused to look at it. Immediately, suspicion flared. Her last stepfather, Sheldon Ferris, had once tried to get money out of her, but Mario had threatened him with the police.

As she checked around the sitting room, she noted that her TV and stereo were still in place, but her laptop was gone.

Kyle terminated the call he'd just made. "A cruiser will be here in the next ten minutes." He frowned. "Did you set the alarm?"

"Before I left. I always do."

While Kyle checked her alarm system, she stepped into her bedroom. Her shocked disbelief was swamped by burning outrage. If her lounge was a mess, her bedroom was worse. Her closet and every drawer had been emptied. Clothes had been dumped on the floor with hangers still attached. Shoes, makeup and costume jewelry were scattered over the bed and the floor. She picked up lacy scraps of underwear and jammed them back in their drawer. She knew she shouldn't touch anything, because the police needed to see the scene of the crime, but she drew the line at having uniformed police officers claiming her underwear as evidence.

Until that moment, she had thought a burglary was about the scariness of a stranger, losing stuff and the inconvenience of insurance claims, but she knew now that wasn't so at all. Shock and anger that someone had thought they had the right to invade her privacy and rummage through her private things kept running through her in waves. They had tossed items aside and taken what they wanted as if she didn't matter.

She didn't know what was missing other than her laptop, but suddenly the laptop ceased to matter. A chill went through her, and she found herself rubbing her arms. Her home, her sanctuary and all of the personal things that were about *her* had been violated.

Kyle, who had been quietly checking through rooms, reappeared and looked annoyed when she told him the laptop was gone. "Anything else appear to be missing?"

She skimmed the room and tried to think, although when her gaze snagged on a broken music box, a precious keepsake from her childhood, her temper soared again. If it was Sheldon, a one-time used car salesman and inveterate swindler, he would know how precious that music box was to her. "It's a little hard to say with all the mess."

His gaze was cool and very steady as he noted the damage. "Made any enemies lately?"

She frowned. "I haven't had time. I work too hard."

"What about in business?"

"I deal with hotel groups and caterers. All they want from me is a confirmed date and a check, which they get."

She heard a car pull into her driveway. Trying to keep her emotions in check, Eva looked through the rooms of her house, relieved to see that the burglar hadn't managed to get to her spare room or the kitchen. Minutes later, she opened the front door for two police officers.

Absently, she noticed that the fresh-faced detectives who introduced themselves as Hicks and Braithewaite seemed dazzled, making her aware that her damp dress was clinging and her hair was tousled. It was a reaction she'd gotten used to over the years, and which she usually managed to ignore.

As Hicks flashed his ID, Kyle stepped into the hall, his hand settling in the small of her back. The small proprietorial touch in front of Hicks forcibly brought back the passionate interlude on the beach. But, given her shakiness over the break-in, she didn't mind the context. Messena and Atraeus men were naturally protective of the women in the family. Whether it was an elderly aunt or someone much younger, the small courtesies and the masculine backup were always available if there was a problem.

Kyle kept her close as Hicks asked questions and looked around. When they walked through the rooms, he even threaded his fingers with hers. They had made love, that was intimate enough, but Kyle's possessive behavior had shunted them straight into something scarily close to coupledom.

Eva's stomach lurched as, once again, she turned over her options: marriage or stay single and possibly lose her business and house, both of which were mortgaged. She faced losing everything for which she had worked so hard over the years. She would survive; she didn't have to have the silk cushion. What would hurt, though, with Mario gone and no inheritance until she was forty, was the feeling of alienation that would go with losing that essential link. Maybe that was a ridiculous way to feel, since she was still an Atraeus by name. But it was a fact that she had always had to strive to fit in, to feel good enough to be an Atraeus.

Whichever way she viewed the future, she kept coming up against one constant: she did not want to cut Kyle out of it. That meant marriage.

She drew a quick breath at a heated flash of their lovemaking. And if what had happened tonight was anything to go on, if they married, even if they started out as a paper marriage, she didn't think it would stay that way.

After taking photographs, Hicks asked a few straightforward questions and made arrangements for an evidence tech to call in and dust for prints in the morning. Eva gave him a description of the laptop and a serial number, and promised to call in to Auckland Central Police Station with a list of anything else that was missing.

She decided against telling him right away about her suspicion that the perpetrator could have been Ferris. If it was, and he had left prints, the police would soon know, anyway, and that meant she got to hold on to her privacy. Mario had been the only member of the family who had known the whole sad and sordid truth about her past, and she preferred to keep it that way.

If Ferris had broken in, his motive would likely be the same as last time. He wanted money, and he wasn't averse to using blackmail to get it. Now that she was quite well known, thanks to her modeling career, he would no doubt threaten to release the details of her disorder and her past to the press.

After closing the door on the detectives, she walked through to the sitting room, where Kyle was examining the photo of her parents where it lay on the table. "Your mother and father?"

"Before they split up." Before her twin had died. Before her father, after finding out about the disorder, had left for Australia and a new life. And before her mother had remarried twice, having children who died to other men who left. Before Eva had discovered that she carried the same rare gene as her mother, a disorder that was lethal for fifty percent of children born to a carrier. In Eva's mother's case, the odds had turned out to be even worse, because out of four children, Eva had been the only one who had survived.

Kyle rose to his feet. "Do you stay in touch with any of your old family?"

The way he said old family, as if he saw her as part of

her new family, the Atraeus clan, was warming. "There was never much family to begin with. My mother was an only child." And the distant family that had been left hadn't wanted to know. "Why do you think I had to be adopted?"

Needing something to do, anything to take her mind off Kyle's large, distracting presence in her house and the tension that seemed to be pulling tighter and tighter, Eva began picking up cushions and stacking them on couches. Given that the cushions were cotton and linen, she figured there was no possibility that they would retain fingerprints. "I haven't seen or spoken with anyone from my mother's family since Mario adopted me."

Kyle began helping her clean up. Thirty minutes later, after picking up all of the loose clothes and underwear and putting them in a laundry basket so they didn't smear any prints that might be on the drawers or closet doors, Eva was satisfied they had done everything they could. She probably should have left everything as it was, but she had needed to restore as much as she could to reclaim her space and counter the creepy knowledge that someone had gotten into her house, even with the alarm turned on.

Kyle checked that the rear door was locked, then extracted his car keys from his pocket. "You can't stay here until you get the locks checked and your alarm upgraded. At a guess, the thief had a piece of equipment that could connect to your alarm wirelessly and give him the code—they're common enough. It would have taken him seconds to break in and then disable the alarm."

A shudder went down her spine at the brief description of how vulnerable she had been in her own home, even with the doors locked. Until she'd given the house a security upgrade, she wouldn't be able to relax, let alone sleep here.

Eva found her cell in her bag. Her first impulse was to ring one of Kyle's twin sisters, either Sophie or Francesca. Unfortunately, both of them had been out of town for a week or so. She checked through her contacts and found a number. "I've got a friend who helps me out at work occasionally. She'll put me up for the night." Annie had once had her own wedding event business, but had segued into special event planning for hotels and major corporations.

Her call went through to Annie's answering service. She tried again, with the same result. She tried Jacinta's number. Normally she never mixed business with her personal life, but she was desperate.

Jacinta's breathless *hello* was cut off by a lazily amused masculine voice, informing her that Jacinta was busy. Cheeks burning, Eva terminated the call.

Kyle lifted a brow. "No luck?"

She reached for her laptop then remembered it had been stolen. Luckily, all of her carefully managed business systems and contact lists were stored remotely so she could retrieve them, but it was still a major inconvenience. She picked up her phone and began looking online for a motel. "I could get a motel."

"Suit yourself. Or you could stay at my place. I've got a house just a couple of minutes from here. There's a guest room."

Tension zinged through her at the thought of staying with Kyle. *And continuing on with what they had started at the beach.* "I didn't know you bought a house." The last she'd heard, Kyle had lived in an ultraexpensive penthouse apartment in the Viaduct, an affluent waterfront area a stone's throw from the center of the city. Although, with all of the frustration of Mario's will and the times she'd had to spend trying to find a husband, she hadn't exactly kept up with family news.

"I bought the old Huntington place. It came up for auction a few weeks back."

Shock jerked Eva's head up. The Huntington place wasn't just a house. It was a fascinating Edwardian red brick folly situated on a rare acre of grounds that also ran down to a tiny private beach. She had caught glimpses of it from the road, through ornate wrought iron bars as she'd either jogged or walked past. But the ivy-festooned walls that glowed in the afternoon light and the lush garden possessed the kind of irresistible romantic charm that had drawn her like a moth to the flame. When she had seen that it was for sale, she had taken a risk and climbed through the gate. The overgrown gardens and the beach had been so beautiful that if she had been able to marry in time and obtain her inheritance, she would have bought it, regardless of what the house was like. "I can't believe you bought that house."

Especially since she had wanted it. From the first moment she had seen it, something had clutched at her heart. It was the most perfect family home she could imagine, even though she would not be requiring it for that, unless at some point she was able to adopt a child. Her most immediate purpose had been for her wedding business. It had everything for a perfect venue.

Kyle's expression turned wary. "What's wrong now?"

Jaw taut, Eva picked up the overnight bag she had packed and her clutch. Somehow, finding out that he was in possession of *her* house was upsetting. She couldn't quite put her finger on why. Maybe she felt so knocked off balance because for years she had been used to forging her own path, making her own decisions and doing things her way. Now, for the first and only time in her life, she had made love—with Kyle. Added to that, Kyle held the balance of power for the two things she wanted: her inheritance and the dream house.

As much as she wanted to say no about something, she couldn't deny the twisted desire to torture herself by looking around a house she knew would be beautiful and exactly what she wanted.

Seeing the house and knowing she could only have it on Kyle's terms would reinforce all of the reasons she should squash the incomprehensible, fatal attraction that had sneaked up on her.

What was wrong now?

She gave Kyle a cool stare. "Nothing much."

When Kyle tried to take her overnight bag, she kept a steely grip on it and marched to the door. "First you deprive me of my wedding. Now you've bought my house."

Seven

The crowded suburbs of Auckland seemed to disappear as Eva drove her car through the gates of Huntington House, with its stone gateposts and aged and stately magnolias arching overhead. Security lights came on, illuminating the thick tangle of rhododendrons and old-fashioned roses planted cheek by jowl with native *ponga* ferns and drifts of *reinga reinga* lilies.

The house was two-storied and peak roofed, with an array of chimneys that poked up against the night sky, adding to the old-world charm. Apart from more security lights, which illuminated the circular piece of drive before the front porch, the house sat in darkness, enclosed and secret with the thick press of overgrown trees and gardens.

Kyle drove into a garage off to the side. Since she was only here for the few hours that were left before she had to be at work, Eva parked near the front portico. By the time she had grabbed her things and locked the car, lights glowed softly in the downstairs area.

The scent of the sea and the sound of the waves hitting the shore nearby should have been relaxing after the tension of the break-in, except that it gave her another searing flashback of their passionate moments on the beach.

The portico lights came on and Kyle opened the front door wider, stepping out to take her bag from her.

Unwillingly loving Kyle's manners, Eva walked into the foyer, her heels clicking on the marble floor. Directly ahead a stairway curved away in a graceful arc. To one side there was an elegant front parlor and what looked like a series of reception and family rooms. On the other side of the staircase she knew, because she had peered through the windows when she had snuck into the estate previously, that a hall led in the direction of the kitchen and what had probably originally been the servants' quarters.

Eva let out a breath. "It's perfect." As a wedding venue. *As a family home*.

Kyle shrugged and indicated she should follow him. "At the moment it's a museum."

"You don't like it?"

"I wouldn't have bought it if I hadn't liked it. It just needs updating."

He walked into a huge kitchen, which was shabby and badly lit, but which already contained a selection of gleaming stainless steel appliances; fridge, cooktop, microwave and dishwasher. Kyle pointed out a kettle and toaster and a pantry that contained cereals and bread and a few food essentials if she needed to make a hot drink or get breakfast.

He indicated she should follow him up the stairs and showed her an array of bedrooms, finishing up with a large room with a king-size bed that was unmistakably his. He set her overnight bag down in the hallway.

Eva's cell beeped. When she took it from her bag, she saw Hicks's name flash up on the screen. When she answered the call, his voice was curt. Apparently they just had a call from a neighbor of hers to say that a man had been seen in her rear garden. They had just dispatched a cruiser to check it out. His main concern was that she was out of the house and safe.

When Kyle realized it was Hicks, he took the phone and had a terse conversation with the cop before terminating the call and handing her phone back, his expression grim. "You're not going back until whoever broke in is in custody."

"If they can catch him." She'd reached her limit for the night. She felt cold and shaky and couldn't seem to stop the tremor in her hands.

"Hicks is no slug. He's a member of the Armed Offenders Squad—he knows what he's doing."

She rubbed at her arms, which suddenly felt chilled, and couldn't keep the grumpiness out of her voice. "How do you know this stuff?"

"Quite a few former SAS end up in the AOS." He stopped. "Are you all right?"

She tried for a smile. "Of course."

"You don't look it."

A split second later she was in his arms, his hold loose enough that she could pull free if she wanted. As if sensing her tension, or more probably realizing that she was actually shaking, he wrapped her more tightly against him.

Eva took a deep breath, soaking in the burning heat that seemed to blast from Kyle as the horrible tension that had crept up on her finally began to unravel. "I guess that's what they call delayed shock. Interesting."

"You can be sure that whoever broke in to your house won't do it again," Kyle said coldly. "I'll make sure of it."

The soft, flat statement sent an electrifying shiver down her spine, and she had a moment to feel sorry for whoever it was who had broken into her house. She tilted her head back and met Kyle's gaze, and just like that her decision was made. Kyle was a powerful, in-control kind of guy, and right now that was exactly what she needed. She would probably regret it, but for better or worse she was going to marry him.

Kyle loosened off his hold slightly. "What is it?"

She drew a deep breath. "You were showing me to my room."

"You can have your own room, or you can share mine. Your choice."

She held his gaze unblinkingly. "Your room."

A hot pang went through her as he cupped her chin and bent his head, giving her plenty of time to pull free if she didn't want the kiss, and abruptly that was the final reassurance she needed. Kyle had already proved that he would never push her where she didn't want to go. Her heart slammed against the wall of her chest as his mouth settled on hers.

Eleven years ago, kissing Kyle had been the angst-filled, desperate risk of a teenager. Now it was an adult reaching for something that had been missing for more years than she cared to count, a hunger for warmth and closeness and for the no-holds-barred intimacy of making love.

Another long, drugging kiss later and she found herself being maneuvered through the door to Kyle's room and walked back in the direction of the bed. But when

Kyle tried to pull free, she coiled her arms around his neck, lifted up and kissed him again.

With a groan he pulled her close. He kissed her, his mouth firm, the feel of his muscled body pressed against hers, the shape of his arousal, the taste of him making her head spin. Another long, heated kiss and she felt her zipper open and the straps of her dress slide from her shoulders. "I'm still sticky and grainy from the beach."

"We can have a shower. Later." As her bra released, she tugged at the buttons of his shirt, dragging it open, but had to stop when he bent and took one breast into his mouth.

Her breath caught in her throat as a heated, aching tension gathered in the pit of her stomach. Somewhere in the distance she heard the lonely sound of a night bird, almost swamped by the slow sound of rain starting on the roof. She arched restlessly against Kyle's mouth, needing something more, but at that point he lifted his head and she felt the soft brush of the bed at the back of her knees. Sliding her hand down over the hard muscle of his abs, she found the top button of his pants, fumbled it open and dragged the zipper down.

Kyle's breath caught audibly, his hand stayed hers. Gaze locked with his, she lifted up and kissed him again. Attempting to step out of her shoes mid-kiss, she wavered off balance and ended up tumbling back on the bed. Kyle sprawled heavily, half on top of her, but when he would have moved, she wound her arms around his neck, tangling her fingers in his dark, silky hair and pressed herself against him.

Acting on impulse, she closed her teeth over the lobe of his ear.

Kyle's fingers closed around her wrists, his breath mingled with hers. "Babe, you don't know what you're—"

"Yes. I do." Dizzy with delight at the feminine power she had over Kyle, stunned by the sensations cascading through her and the careful way he held her close as if he truly cared for her, she kissed him again.

She felt his swiftly indrawn breath. "This time we're doing it right."

He disentangled himself and obtained a foil packet from his bedside table. After sheathing himself, he returned to the bed. A split second later, his weight came down on hers.

He cupped her face. "Are you sure you want to do this again?"

She lifted up for his kiss. "Why would there be a problem?"

She felt the scrape of lace as he peeled her panties down her legs, then his thighs parted hers. "Correct me if I'm wrong, but I think it's been a while since you've done this."

She hesitated, on the brink of telling him that before tonight she had never "done this," but then a quiet, instinctive caution gripped her. She had already given more of herself, and agreed to more, than she had planned. The urge to protect herself now was knee-jerk. Confessing that until tonight she had been a virgin would lay bare too much.

This time their lovemaking was more leisurely as he took his time kissing her, cupping her breasts and at the same time encouraging her to explore. Just when she thought she couldn't take much more play, she felt the press of him between her legs. Automatically, she shifted to accommodate him.

This time their joining was smoother, easier. She heard his indrawn breath, then his mouth came down on hers and he began to move and the heated tension turned molten.

Long minutes later, Kyle gently disengaged himself and rolled to one side, taking her with him.

There was a small vibrating silence. "The condom slipped the first time, but that's never happened before, so there's no risk of STDs" He propped himself up on one elbow. "But you also should have told me you haven't made love for a while."

She studied the stubbled line of his jaw, and the resolve not to reveal just how vulnerable she was with all things sexual settled in. She ran her palm over the damp skin of his chest, and evaded his gaze. "There wasn't exactly much time for conversation."

He cupped one breast, the intimate touch sending a tingling thrill through her. "It would have been good to know. We could have done things…differently."

She shivered as he dipped down and took her nipple in his mouth, her eyes closing as the heated, coiling tension started all over again. She tried to think, but her brain was fast becoming scrambled. "How, exactly?"

"I would have taken a whole lot more time."

Her eyes flipped open at the way his voice cooled, as if he was remembering the mishap with the condom. She summoned as much confidence as she could. "There won't be a baby."

Although the gravity of what had happened came back to hit her full force. The plain fact was that because she hadn't been sexually active, she didn't know a lot about where in her cycle was the optimum time to get pregnant. She had never before needed to keep track of her ovulation. She knew roughly when her period was, but that was about it. If by some remote chance she did get pregnant… But that wouldn't happen, she thought grimly, she would make sure of it. She would make an appointment to see her doctor tomorrow and get a morning-after pill.

And arrange contraception.

The decision made, she forced herself to relax about the whole issue of pregnancy. There was nothing she could do until the morning. "I'm sorry we didn't have a conversation before we made love, but I thought if we stopped you might…leave." She lifted up, pressing against his chest, and boldly rolled on top. "It's not as if you haven't done that before."

He tangled his hands in her hair, grinned lazily and pulled her mouth down to his. "You must be talking about leaving, since we've never made love before."

He kissed her and she felt him stir against her stomach. He rolled until they were lying comfortably sprawled, side by side.

It occurred to Eva that she had never felt so relaxed or so comfortable with a man, and she went still inside at the stunning thought that since Kyle didn't want kids then maybe, just maybe, he was the perfect man for her?

Just as long as she didn't get pregnant.

Eva woke to the sound of the shower. She blinked at the enormous old-fashioned room with its striped brown wallpaper and bare boards. She was presently the sole occupant of the huge modern bed, which sat in the center of the room.

Kyle stepped back into the room, wearing dark pants and a shirt he was in the process of buttoning. Feeling exposed, Eva dragged the sheet up to her chin before attempting to drape the sheet around her like a sarong.

Kyle strapped on his watch. "We need to have a conversation before we go to work."

Eva tried for a smile as if waking up in some man's bed after spur-of-the-moment sex was a very normal thing for her. "A conversation would be good in just a few minutes."

She found her overnight bag and lugged it through to the bathroom, which was still steamy from Kyle's occupancy. She quickly showered and dressed. There was no dryer, so she had to be content with combing her hair out straight. She quickly made up her face then checked her appearance. When she saw a faint pink graze on her neck, where Kyle's five-o'clock shadow must have scraped against her skin, the reality of what they'd done last night hit her.

When Kyle knocked on the door, she stuffed the sheet she'd worn into a laundry basket, hung up her towel and walked out into the hall. She was still barefoot, and Kyle, now fully dressed in a dark suit with a blue tie that made his eyes seem even bluer, towered over her.

She had hoped he might pull her into his arms and kiss her so they could both relax and have the discussion they needed to have, but he had his banker face on, cool, neutral and unreadable.

He glanced at his watch. "If we're going to get married, we should make arrangements."

Eva frowned at the way Kyle had casually leapfrogged the whole concept of a proposal. She guessed it wasn't warranted in her case, because she was the one seeking the marriage. Technically, Kyle was doing her the favor, but he had *checked his watch* as if he didn't even have time to talk about it.

Abruptly, she wondered if their lovemaking last night had meant anything at all to him. Annoyed enough to keep him waiting, Eva reached into her bag and found her cell, taking her time as she flicked through to her calendar, which she already knew was packed full of consultations that morning and clear for most of the afternoon, which meant she could book a doctor's appointment directly after lunch.

His gaze shifted to her mouth, and for a shivering moment the sensual tension was alive between them.

"What's wrong?"

"That would be the marriage thing. You haven't exactly asked me."

There was a vibrating silence. "I thought I had."

With careful precision, Eva checked the next month's appointments, of which, thankfully, there were a number. "I can recall something along the lines of a command, followed by a business-type proposition."

"Correct me if I'm wrong, but technically it *is* a business proposition. If you become engaged to me, the marriage can be approved immediately, since Mario made it clear his first preference for a husband was a Messena. You should have access to your trust fund within a couple of weeks. After two years, you receive the full inheritance."

When she continued to flick fruitlessly through her calendar, Kyle said something soft and curt beneath his breath. They both knew her answer had to be yes, but she was frustrated and terminally annoyed that after the searing intimacy they'd shared last night, he was now treating her as if she was an irritating pain in the rear again.

"Marry me, and you get the house."

She clamped down on the automatic burst of outrage that Kyle clearly thought she was so materialistic that he could buy her with the house. "I thought you bought the house for yourself."

He straightened away from the doorframe, but still didn't enter the bedroom, his expression oddly cagey. "For the short term. It's a good investment."

It occurred to Eva that after the passionate lovemaking last night, Kyle was now doing his level best to create some distance. Maybe it was just a masculine desire to compartmentalize. Whatever it was, it did not work for her. The last thing she wanted was to be treated as some kind of sexual convenience who could be bought.

She drew a deep breath. "Okay, I'll marry you. But what happened last night can't happen again. If you want a marriage of convenience then it has to be on the same terms I offered the others."

She hated saying the words; she had adored making love with Kyle, and she wanted to do it again but she couldn't do so under these conditions.

The hum of a cell sounded from his jacket. The cool neutrality of his expression, the same kind of expression she imagined he used at the negotiating table, didn't alter. "No sex. Agreed."

Kyle reached for his cell and slid smoothly into a business conversation, but Eva refused to let herself get either angry or depressed about it. Last night had been special in a way she hadn't expected, but this morning they had bounced back into the old, aggravated relationship. But perhaps the fact that Kyle had pressed her for marriage signaled that he wasn't as indifferent as he seemed.

It shouldn't be important, but she had to wonder exactly how Kyle had viewed their night together, her first and only night with a man. According to the gossip columnists, like all the ultrawealthy Messena and Atraeus men, he was hotly pursued and had enjoyed a number of brief liaisons. And, of course, she could not forget that he had been married. On his scale of things, having sex with her had probably barely registered.

Kyle terminated the call. "I'll apply for the marriage license today. How about having the wedding the week after next? Thursday?"

The date he wanted was twelve days away. She had already checked her calendar, so she knew that day was free. "Are you sure it has to be a Thursday?" Who got married on a Thursday?

She did. Giddy pleasure fizzed through her, which was crazy and dangerous, because she could not afford to project any kind of romanticism into this *business deal*. She could not afford to make herself any more vulnerable to Kyle than she already was.

Kyle leaned against the door, his gaze lingering on the rumpled bed. "You can change the date if you want. I'll just have to check in with my PA."

"Thursday will do." At least it would mean she would have more chance of getting a venue she liked, because all the good ones would be booked out on a weekend day.

"And Eva?"

She tried for her absentminded "I'm concentrating so hard on my schedule that I can't hear you" look, although from the piercing quality of Kyle's gaze she wasn't entirely sure she pulled it off. "What?"

"We need to keep the wedding low-key."

"What exactly do you mean by low-key?"

"I was thinking a registry office, two witnesses."

She stiffened as it occurred to her that while Kyle hadn't minded sleeping with her, he was not entirely happy at being linked with her in marriage. That maybe marrying a lingerie model did not fit so well with his conservative banker's image.

She tucked her cell back in her bag. "Maybe the word you should have used to describe the wedding is *secret*?"

"There's not exactly time for a big wedding."

"And why would we have one when it's only for two years?"

A pulse started along the side of his jaw. "Precisely."

She forced a smooth, professional smile. "No problem. We can get married *quietly*."

But it would not be in a registry office, and it would not be a hole-in-the-corner affair, as if Kyle was ashamed to be marrying her!

Eight

Shortly after nine that morning, Kyle's twin sisters, Sophie and Francesca, who had both recently returned from a buying trip for Sophie's boutique in Australia, cornered him at his favorite café. It was a neat pincer operation that could only have been spearheaded by his mother, whom he had made the mistake of ringing before he had left the house for work. Sophie, who was normally sleek and unruffled, looked haphazard in jeans and a cotton sweater, as if she'd left the house in a hurry. Francesca, the more flamboyant of the two, looked pale and still half-asleep.

Kyle braced himself. Both twins worked some distance away, and thus they did not normally frequent this café, which was close to his bank. He loved his sisters, they had stood by him through thick and thin, but they had a take-charge streak and a facility for winkling out the truth that tended to make things worse. "What do you want?"

Sophie lifted a brow. "We're family. Maybe we just saw you and wanted to say hello?"

Resigned, Kyle paid for his coffee and ordered a long black for Sophie, a latte for Francesca. "I repeat, what do you want?"

Sophie gave him a serene look. "Mom rang. We know you're engaged to Eva—we want to know why. You know we love you, Kyle. We also love Eva. Just answer our questions and we'll let you go."

Kyle paid for the coffees and joined Sophie and Francesca, who had commandeered a corner table. "Maybe we fell in love."

Neither of the twins showed a flicker of interest in his reply. Resigning himself to a longer conversation, Kyle sat back and worked on his poker face.

Their coffee arrived. After the waitress had gone, Francesca leaned forward and gave him a friendly smile. "You kissed Eva on the beach approximately eleven years ago, since then, nothing." She made a slitting motion across her throat. *"Niente."*

Kyle didn't allow his sister's Italian theatrics to do what they were designed to do—lure him into a discussion about his love life so they could really mess with his head. He had no idea how the twins had found out that piece of information, since he hadn't told anyone, including his mother. To his certain knowledge, the only people who had known had been Mario, who was now dead, and Eva. "Since I know you're not psychic, so you couldn't have spoken to Mario, I'm guessing you talked to Eva."

Sophie set her coffee down. "She rang me first thing. She needs a dress."

Kyle pinched his nose. The phone had obviously been running red hot.

A dress. That did not sound like a registry office wedding. "And since you supply a lot of Eva's brides, she called you."

"It's good business. I recommend Eva's wedding planning. She recommends my dresses. It's a marriage made in heaven," Sophie said smoothly, "while this one, clearly, is not."

Francesca put her coffee down with a snap. "We know Eva needs a husband to get her inheritance."

The hum of conversation in the café abruptly dropped. Heads began to swivel. Kyle's jaw compressed. "Eva told you that?"

Francesca blushed. "Not exactly. I saw Mario's will on your coffee table in your apartment one day. I couldn't help wondering why you even had a copy, so—"

"You read a confidential document."

Francesca's brows jerked together. "Maybe you shouldn't have left it out where just anyone could read it."

Kyle could have pointed out that his apartment wasn't exactly a public area, but he recognized a blind ally when he saw one. A little desperately he tried to recall the original thread of the conversation. "The reason I'm marrying Eva is private and, uh, personal."

A hot flash of just how private and personal they had gotten last night momentarily distracted him. He dragged at his tie, which suddenly felt a little tight, then realized his mistake when Sophie noticed the faint red mark on the side of his neck.

Sophie blinked. "You're sleeping with her. That changes things."

Francesca stared at him as if he'd just grown horns. "You're Eva's legal trustee and you're *sleeping* with her? Aside from being sleazy, isn't that against the law?"

Kyle kept a firm grip on his temper. "I'm not responsible for Eva. I'm a trustee of her adoptive father's will, that's an entirely different thing—"

Francesca gave him a horrified look. "Then she's pregnant."

"She can't be pregnant." Although the thought hit him like a hammer blow, despite Eva's confidence that she couldn't be.

He took a mouthful of coffee, which he suddenly needed. Although, Eva had not seemed to be worried about the possibility of a pregnancy, so he assumed that, like a lot of women, she was on the pill or had taken some other precaution.

Another thought hit him out of the blue as the strange dichotomy of making love with a sophisticated woman who had been at turns fiery and passionate then oddly awkward and uncertain registered. He had assumed the reason Eva had been awkward and uncertain was that she hadn't made love for a very long time.

Either that, or she was a virgin.

He drew a long breath and let it out slowly. He knew that Eva had never had a live-in lover; that was common family knowledge. They had all assumed it was because Mario was so old-fashioned and that Eva, out of respect for her adoptive father, was preserving an outward show of chastity. It had never occurred to any of them, least of all, Kyle, that she had been doing exactly what it appeared; keeping herself for marriage.

Although, technically, she hadn't saved herself for her wedding night.

"So this is going to be a real marriage?" Sophie picked up her bag, which she'd placed on the floor.

Kyle frowned as Sophie extracted her phone and made a call, speaking in the kind of low, flat voice that could have been lifted straight out of some B-grade thriller.

Apparently, something was green, not red, the 10-33 was over but in general it all still qualified as Alpha Charlie Foxtrot.

Kyle recognized code when he heard it, even if it was a crazy mix of the standard radio language used by the military for decades and the 10 Code that was in popular use by police and emergency services. At a strong guess she was relaying information to their mom, who had spent time volunteering for the local ambulance service as one of their call operators. "If you hand the phone to me, I can speak to Mom direct."

Sophie's gave him a faintly irritated look. "No need. She'll be in Auckland by this afternoon. You can talk to her at my apartment, since both you and Eva are invited to dinner at my place tonight. There's a lot to decide in a short time frame."

"Not that much, since the wedding is in twelve day's time."

Francesca gave him a pitying look. "You're marrying a wedding planner. They're Type As. And you know, Eva, she's like a double A."

Sophie set her cup down. "That means perfectionist. Aggressive. Even if you got married in a registry office, which will never happen because I know what the dress is going to be, it would be the most perfect registry office wedding imaginable. But, like I said, it's not a registry office, so you should brace yourself."

Kyle groaned inwardly. When he'd left Eva that morning, he'd been relieved that he'd gotten her to agree to the marriage. His concern had been to get the marriage done quickly and quietly. He thought he'd managed to convey that to Eva, but something must have gotten lost in translation, because now all hell was breaking loose.

But now he could see he had made a big mistake in

not factoring in the impact this would have on his family. Mistakenly, he had assumed that his mother, who had been pressurizing him to think about marriage again and find someone "nice," would be happy that he had finally decided to step back into relationship waters again.

The certainty that Eva had been a virgin when they had made love hit him anew. The anomaly of Eva choosing to give herself to him after years of celibacy and before they had even agreed to a marriage pointed to only one clear answer.

She wanted him just as badly as he wanted her.

An odd tension dissipated at the thought. At the same time, Kyle was aware that hell would probably freeze over before Eva would admit feeling anything at all for him. But then Mario had given him the distinct impression that Eva had suffered a lot of emotional difficulties as a child. He had assumed there was abuse in her past and had done what Mario requested and left her alone. He hadn't pried into Eva's history, but now that they were getting married, he resolved to find out exactly what had gone wrong.

A part of him was fiercely glad that Eva hadn't slept around, that she had waited and given herself to him. But he was aware that he would have to step carefully. He was cool, logical and disciplined. Eva was gorgeous and passionate, like rich, decadent chocolate, meant to be enjoyed in small, ruthlessly measured doses.

Francesca waved a hand in front of his face to attract his attention. "Just tell us one thing. Is Eva pressuring you to marry her?"

"No." The reason he wanted to marry Eva was cut and dried: it was the most efficient way of keeping her away from other men.

Sophie gave him a considering look. "But this is a marriage of convenience, right?"

Kyle decided there was no point prevaricating, since the twins had clearly made up their minds that it was. "Yes."

Sophie stared at him with her spooky eyes, the ones that interrogation officers would kill for and which sucked the truth out of you whether you wanted to tell or not. Clearly, she had just sucked something significant out of his brain, because she exchanged a look with Francesca. "Is there something wrong with a marriage of convenience?"

The twins gave him a pitying look.

Sophie sat back in her chair as if the case was concluded. "A marriage of convenience where you sleep with Eva? Sounds like a real marriage to us."

Eva rushed to her doctor's appointment only to find her last consultation had dragged on so long she had missed it and had to wait for an emergency appointment. Stomach churning, not least because she hadn't stopped to get any lunch, she sat down to wait.

At three o'clock, she finally got in to see Dr. Evelyn Shan, an elegant Indian woman with an impressive list of qualifications and a daughter, Lina, who had been a good friend of Eva's in her last year of school.

After a couple of minutes of catching up about Lina, who now lived in England, Eva finally managed to get to the point of her visit.

Evelyn's eyes widened ever so slightly at Eva's request for morning-after and contraceptive pills, before she began asking a crisp series of questions. "I'll prescribe the morning-after pill, and you need to take it today, as soon as possible. The results aren't one hundred percent, and given the time in your cycle…"

She scribbled a prescription. Eva, feeling about six inches tall, folded the piece of paper and placed it in her handbag. As she hurried out to pay for the consultation, her phone vibrated.

She took the call from Luisa Messena, Kyle's mother. Feeling frazzled, she agreed to meet Luisa, Francesca and Sophie at a nearby café in a few minutes, although she was certain "coffee" was a euphemism for what was about to take place. As much as she loved the Messena women and enjoyed their company, they were, each in their own way, formidable. It was also a fact that the twins knew about the clause in Mario's will.

She paid and filled her prescription at a chemist then hurried to the café. Sophie and Francesca were grinning like a couple of cats that had gotten the cream. Luisa hugged her with an odd smile in her eyes.

Feeling dazed that all three women seemed quite relaxed about the quick marriage, Eva ordered sparkling water. She intended to sip some now then cap the bottle, place it in her bag and, as soon as she got a chance, take her pill. She didn't want to risk taking the pill at the table, because she was pretty sure that if she took out the pack, the twins would recognize the medication and all hell would break loose.

Half an hour later, just as she was making her excuses to leave, Detective Hicks called. They needed to get into her house to dust for fingerprints, and they needed her to meet them there now.

After quickly explaining about the break-in to Luisa, Sophie and Francesca, she got up to leave, but Luisa wouldn't hear about her going on her own and insisted on calling Kyle.

She beamed as she disconnected the call. "He's more or less finished for the day and will drive you to your house."

Feeling just a little bit frantic because she needed a few minutes alone to take the pill, Eva found herself strolling across the road to Kyle's bank, an imposing old building with several floors and a plaster facade in a tasteful shade of mocha. She stepped through antique wood-and-glass revolving doors into the hushed echoes of a large reception area with marble floors and very high, intricately molded ceilings. She had been in the bank on a number of occasions before, but always with Mario.

Kyle stepped out of an elevator, and her heart did a queer little leap. He was dressed in the same suit she had seen him wearing that morning, *after she had gotten out of his bed*, but he looked...different. Maybe it was the understated richness of marble floors and pillars, the diffused light that shimmered through fanlights over the doors, but in that moment he looked utterly at home in the opulence and wealth of the bank and every inch the urban predator.

An hour later, they left her house, locking it behind the police team. After the short drive home, where they were changing for dinner because they were eating out, Eva finally made it to a bathroom.

Setting her bag down on the vanity, she took the morning-after pill out of her bag and read the instructions.

She needed to take the pill in the first twenty-four hours. She checked her watch. She was within the time.

Relief making her a little dizzy, she filled a glass with water, popped the pill in her mouth, took a mouthful of water and swallowed.

Nine

Ten days later, Eva walked into her office to find Jacinta rushing out, her normally magnolia cheeks bright pink. "Anything wrong?"

"Nothing." Jacinta waved her clipboard. "Just needed this. I must have left it in here by mistake. Oh, and some man called to see you. I actually found him in your office when I came in with coffee and shooed him out. I noted down his number on the pad beside your phone."

Frowning that someone had walked into her office while she'd been having a fitting for her dress at Sophie's shop, and without an appointment, Eva checked out the number, which was unfamiliar.

Eva sat down behind her desk. It was then she noticed that her handbag, which she'd left behind because Sophie's shop was just down the street, was gaping open. Mario's will was tucked inside where she had left it, but she couldn't remember it being folded open at the second page.

Feeling unsettled, she refolded the will and replaced it in her bag. It was ridiculous to think that the person in her office could be Sheldon Ferris. Picking up the phone, she rang the cell number noted on the pad.

A male voice picked up, and her stomach plummeted as she recognized her stepfather's voice. "What were you doing in my office?"

"Now, what way is that to talk to a relative? Especially with a wedding coming up."

The veiled threat in his voice made her tense. "You married my mother for a couple of years. That doesn't make you a relative."

"I suppose, now you're an Atraeus, and rich, you've got no time for the family you left behind—"

"If you want money, you can forget it." As far as she was concerned, Ferris had only ever been with her mother to benefit himself. He had lived off her sickness benefit and run up enough gambling debts that when her mother had died there had been nothing left.

There was a small silence. "You're not going to get rid of me this time." He mentioned a figure that took her breath. "If you don't want your story splashed all over the tabloids, you'd better pay up."

In that moment Eva noticed a message sitting on her blotter, from Detective Hicks, to the effect that they hadn't been able to make a positive ID on any finger-prints other than her own. She didn't care, she was now sure in her own mind who it was that had broken in. "That was you in my house the other night, wasn't it?"

The click of the disconnected call in her ear was loud enough that she wrenched the phone away. With shaky fingers, she set the phone down in its rest.

Sheldon Ferris. He popped up in her life at odd inter-vals, usually wanting money. Mario had frightened him off the last time, but Mario had failed to tell her what leverage he had used. All she could hope was that the fear of a police investigation would be enough to scare him off.

With the pleasure of trying on her wedding dress drained away by the nasty call, Eva deliberately tried to recapture her optimistic mood by checking through her wedding file.

Predictably, Kyle had not been happy when he'd discovered that Eva had not booked a registry office wedding and that she had involved Kyle's family in almost every aspect. Eva, on the other hand, had felt it was important that his family were involved, not least because in a more distant way, they were also her family.

She had invited the Messena clan to her last wedding, which hadn't happened, so why would she not invite them to this one, especially when Kyle was the groom? It just hadn't made any kind of sense to cut family out and in the process cause hurt.

It still felt faintly surreal that she was actually getting married, and that the toxic clause in Mario's will would be neutralized in just two days' time.

Two days until she became Kyle's wife.

The speed with which the wedding was approaching made her feel breathless and just a little panicky, which was not her. Usually she was in control and organized. She lived and breathed detail and was superpicky about every aspect of a wedding, which made her good at her job. She also had a huge network of contacts thanks to her family and her modeling days. She had thought twelve days was enough time to organize a small, intimate wedding, but it seemed the universe was working against her.

She'd fought tooth and nail over venues, food and music, and she was losing sleep. To cap it off, none of her bridesmaids of choice were available on a Thursday. Even Sophie and Francesca had had prior commitments that meant that, while they could come to the wedding, they just did not have enough time to do all the bridesmaid things. She was starting to get desperate. The way things were going, the wedding *would* take place in a registry office.

Jacinta strolled back in with the clipboard in her hand, this time with a couple of sheets attached. Her dark bob was perfect and glossy, her vivid pink cotton dress, cinched in at the waist, made her honey tan look even darker and more exotic. "You said you wanted to talk to me about a new wedding."

Eva slid the page with the basic plan she had arrived at across her desk. "It's my wedding."

Her eyes widened with shock. "But, since Jeremy went to Dubai, you're not even going out with anyone—unless Troy Kendal proposed?"

"Uh-uh. Not Troy." Eva tried to look unconcerned and very busy shuffling pieces of paper as Jacinta flipped the sheet around and stared at the line that contained the groom's name.

"You're marrying Kyle Messena?" There was a curious silence. "Now I am confused. He's a babe, but I didn't think you even liked him."

Eva avoided Jacinta's curious gaze and tried to look serenely in love, which was difficult because nothing she felt for Kyle fell into the "serene" bracket. "*Like* doesn't exactly describe what I feel for Kyle."

That, at least, was honest. Nothing about any of their interactions had ever fallen into comfortable friendship territory. "We had a *thing* years ago, and when he knew how close I came to marrying Jeremy, he, uh…decided we should be together."

Jacinta managed to morph surprise into sparkly enthusiasm. "Sounds take-charge and…romantic."

Eva caught the subtext, *and so not like Eva*. She searched for a little enthusiasm herself. "Like I said, we go way back."

Desperate to quit the conversation, she checked her wristwatch. Happily, she had arranged to have lunch with Kyle, so she had a legitimate out. Jumping to her feet, she hooked the strap of the sleek handbag over her shoulder. "You know," she said vaguely, "the family connection."

Jacinta added the sheet to her file, her expression vaguely horrified. "Of course. If he's a Messena, then you're related."

Eva frowned at the way she said it. "The connection is hardly close. Mario was Kyle's great-uncle, and don't forget that I'm adopted."

"It's coming back."

Eva forced a smile. "Which reminds me, I have a favor to ask. We want to get married this week, and I was wondering if you could be my bridesmaid?"

"This week?"

"Thursday." She caught another little piece of subtext. "I'll supply the dress and shoes from Sophie Messena's boutique."

Jacinta's expression brightened. "Okay." She hugged the clipboard to her stomach. "I guess you must have both discovered you're crazy in love? Like a fatal attraction, since you didn't seem to even like one another at the Hirsch wedding."

Eva's phone chimed, negating the need to answer. Clutching the cell like a lifeline, Eva answered the call, which was from Kyle. She said his name with a pleased smile and waggled her hand at Jacinta, as if this somehow answered the question of whether or not she was in love. Happy to be free from the interrogation, she stepped out of the office.

"You sound happy."

The low register of Kyle's voice brushed across her nerves as she punched the call button of the elevator. She had stuck to her resolve that she and Kyle wouldn't sleep together, but listening to Kyle's voice, which was drop-dead sexy, didn't help. Neither did the fact that Kyle was exhibiting a kind of calm, measured patience with her that was downright scary. She shouldn't like that in an utterly male way he was waiting for her to get back into his bed. "It's lunchtime. I get to eat."

"And I intend to feed you."

Eva's fingers tightened on the phone. Why did that sound so carnal? She stepped into the elevator and hit the button to close the doors. "Where, exactly?"

"It's a surprise. I'll be waiting for you downstairs."

As she stepped out of the elevator, despite giving herself a stern talking-to on the way down, her heart skipped a beat when she saw Kyle. She was glad she had worn one of her favorite dresses, a cream sheath dress that made the best of her honey tan and tawny hair. Kyle was dressed in a sleek, dark suit with a snowy-white shirt and dark red tie and looked edgily handsome and just a little re-mote. She tried to look breezy and casual as she walked toward him, as if making love with him and agreeing to marriage had not been earth-shattering events but, even so, her stomach automatically tightened.

He held the door for her, and she stepped through, sud-denly feeling ridiculously feminine and cosseted. Since the dinner with his mother and sisters, courtesy of liv-ing in the same house, they had spent more time together than she could remember since the Dolphin Bay days, and the tension was wearing on her nerves. "Where are we going?"

He opened the passenger side door of the Maserati and named an exclusive jeweler's. A glow of pleasure infused her. "You don't have to get me a ring."

His gaze touched on hers. "The ring's nonnegotiable. My family will expect it, and so will the media."

Her jaw squared at his reasoning and the quick little dart of hurt that went with it. Just for a moment she had felt that Kyle really did care for her and the engagement meant something more to him than a business arrangement. It was the kind of dangerous thinking she knew she couldn't afford, but which somehow kept materializing. As if it mattered that Kyle should care for her.

As if she wanted this marriage to be real.

Ten

Jaw squaring, Eva slid into her seat. "You don't have to buy the ring. I'll get one for myself, after lunch."

There was a moment of silence before the door closed with an expensive *thunk*. Fingers shaking just a little because out-of-the-blue anger had piled on top of the hurt and all over a piece of jewelry. Kyle slid into the driver's seat as she fastened her seat belt.

Somewhere behind them a horn blared. Glancing in the rearview mirror, she saw a delivery truck waiting for the space that Kyle had illegally commandeered. Her cheeks heated as she became aware that Kyle, aside from starting the car, wasn't moving. "We should go before you get a ticket."

"Not until we get something straight. I buy the ring."

Taking a deep breath, she forced her fingers to loosen on the buttery leather of her bag. "No."

The delivery truck gave another extended blast on its horn.

"I'm not moving until you agree."

She frowned at his steely blue gaze and the rock-hard set of his jaw. Not for the first time, she saw the defining quality that had seen him promoted in the military and which made him such an asset in the banking business: the cold, hard-assed ability to force his own terms.

It passed through her mind that living with Kyle would not be a cakewalk. He would be demanding, opinionated and difficult; she just bet that with his military training, he probably liked to make rules. Irritatingly, it also registered that she could never be happy with a man who didn't challenge her, that a part of her relished the battle. That in some crazy, un-PC way, Kyle suited her and that she would rather argue with him than agree with any other man she knew. "What if I don't want a ring?"

"Sophie said you wanted a dress. Why not the ring?"

She thought quickly. He was right, she did want the ring.

She guessed that, in her heart of hearts, it was tied in with the reason she wanted a real wedding in the first place. She liked the enduring conventions and traditions, the beauty and hopefulness, and she wanted to enjoy the occasion. Somehow, in going through the same process that countless other couples had entered into, there was a comforting sense of being a part of something time-honored and lovely, even if the marriage was a sham.

She decided the timing was right to mention another detail of the wedding preparations. "I'll have the ring, but on the condition that we get married in a church."

Kyle pulled out and let the delivery van take the space. "Let me guess. You've already booked the church."

"Since it's difficult to get one of those at short notice, I booked as soon as I had the date."

The extended silence that accompanied Kyle's smooth

insertion into city traffic underlined the fact that he wasn't happy with the idea of a wedding in a church.

Suddenly incensed, Eva contemplated telling Kyle to pull over so she could get out and walk back to her office. Her shoes were too high, her feet would hurt and she'd probably wilt in the heat, but it would be worth it. "If you think I'm going to stand in some dusty registrar's office somewhere, you can forget it."

Eva backed her statement with a fiery glance, in that moment prepared to cancel the wedding, cancel her very important plans for her business and the gorgeous house of her dreams—all disastrous consequences. It occurred to her that somewhere between sleeping with Kyle and agreeing to marry him she had lost her perspective and was hatching into a fully-fledged bridezilla.

Kyle muttered something curt beneath his breath as he accelerated through an intersection. "Are you always this difficult?"

Eva stared at oncoming traffic, barely seeing it. "You know I am. Mario would have wanted a church wedding. It's important."

"I guess I keep forgetting I'm marrying a wedding planner."

The easy way he said the words as if, ultimately, Kyle was relaxed with the whole idea of marriage and prepared to give her her way, doused the escalating tension. The dress, the ring and getting married in church might seem inconsequential to Kyle, but they mattered to Eva. Her upbringing with Mario had always included the church. In their small family, faith had been central, deep and important. She wouldn't feel married if it wasn't done in a church.

Kyle braked as traffic slowed. "Which church and what time?"

Kyle's sudden change of heart about the church, the ease with which he had adapted, sparked a suspicion. "You knew about the church all along."

"I didn't know the details, but the twins gave me a heads-up."

Which meant, since he hadn't mentioned it before, that he had more than likely saved the knowledge as a bargaining chip. In this case, to make sure she had the engagement ring he wanted to give her.

Feeling suddenly, blazingly happy that he had gone to so much trouble for her, she gave him the details. "It's the little church just down from the house. I was lucky enough to get it at short notice."

The vicar hadn't liked having his arm twisted, since he'd had to reschedule a regular session of the La Leche League, who had their monthly meeting in an adjacent room, but she had doubled the fee, which had smoothed things over.

A bus up ahead stopped for a set of lights. Eva winced as she recognized one of her last lingerie advertisements splashed over the rear of the bus.

The fizzing happiness died a death. Just what she needed, a reminder that Kyle was marrying a woman who was more recognizable to the general population half-naked than fully dressed. And in that moment it hit her what that would mean to a man who made his living in the ultraconservative world of banking. To say that she was an unsuitable wife for a man who dealt with the stiff etiquette of that social world was a massive understatement.

A car peeled right and, as luck would have it, they ended up snug behind the bus, with her airbrushed, overly enhanced cleavage looming large. Eva's fingers tightened on her handbag, as any hope that Kyle had not seen the advertisement faded.

When she had been modeling, the profession had been so competitive that this particular lingerie shoot had seemed a good business move. It had certainly kept her in public view, but until now she had not noticed how tacky the posters were.

Even more on edge now, she stared at Kyle's profile, the clean-cut strength of his jaw and the way his broken nose made him look even sexier. "Maybe you shouldn't marry me."

Kyle's gaze captured hers. "What's wrong now?"

The mild, patient way he asked the question, as if she was a high-maintenance girlfriend *with issues*, made her stiffen. "Won't marrying me be a problem in terms of your career?"

Mario had thrown up his hands often enough at her decision to become a lingerie model. Added to that, over the years Eva had become sharply aware that her career, coupled with the Atraeus name, had guaranteed the kind of prying, intrusive media attention she hated.

Kyle pulled into a reserved space in the crowded, popular enclave that was the Viaduct, a collection of bars and cafés and apartments on the waterfront, just a stone's throw from the central heart of Auckland. Unfastening his seat belt, he half turned to face her, and suddenly the interior of the Maserati seemed suffocatingly small. "Is this about the lingerie ads?"

She met his gaze squarely. "It could affect your business. I mean, won't there be occasions when I have to socialize with some of your clients?"

"Honey, I part own the bank. I can buy and sell most of my clients. If they've got a problem with my wife, they can take their business elsewhere."

A curious tingling sensation riveted her to her seat. As Kyle exited the car, she registered what that sensation was: the recognition that in that moment something basic and utterly primitive had taken place. Without so much as the blink of an eye, Kyle had informed her that she was more important than his business. More, he had given her an assurance that he would uphold her honor and protect her unconditionally. An assurance that was guaranteed to melt her all the way through, because he had made her feel that she belonged to him.

Suddenly, it did not seem like a marriage of convenience to Eva.

Kyle opened her door and held out his hand. Still feeling electrified by the uncompromising way Kyle had stated his solidarity with her, his intention, on the surface of things, to treat her as a real wife, Eva put her hand in his. When she straightened, for a moment she was close enough to Kyle that she could see the crystalline clarity of his irises and the intriguing dark striations, the inky blackness of his lashes.

Only one other person had done the same, and that had been Mario.

She was aware that Kyle would know some of the details of her background, but only the parts that she and Mario had agreed could be known. He did not know about the genetic disorder, the deaths of her brother and sisters and her mother's depression; the constant moves to avoid one of her mother's violent boyfriends. He could not know or guess how difficult it was for her to trust *anyone*.

She had entrusted herself to Kyle, and now she knew why. Somehow, beneath the battle lines they had drawn for so long and all the tension and clashes, she had recognized that bedrock quality in Kyle. It was the same quality that had attracted her when she was seventeen and still raw from the disintegration of her family and being handed through a list of foster homes. It explained why she had never really forgotten him, even though he had walked away.

For a split second, his gaze rested on her mouth, and she realized that in his sharp, percipient way, he had picked up on the intensity of her thoughts and was going to pull her close and kiss her. She was so sure of it that she unconsciously rebalanced her weight to lean in close.

"Kyle! I saw you from across the street. I've been trying to get hold of you."

"Elise. I was going to call you."

Eva stiffened as a tall, narrow brunette with dainty features and a simple silk shift and jacket that she instantly recognized as Chanel, stepped up to Kyle and kissed him on the cheek. The extremity of Eva's reaction was easily recognizable; she was jealous. Why she hadn't considered that Kyle had a girlfriend she didn't know.

Kyle disentangled himself, his expression neutral. His arm came around her as he introduced Elise, a financial consultant with a rival bank. In clipped tones, he introduced Eva as his fiancée.

There was a moment of stony silence, and Eva found it in herself to be sorry for Elise.

Elise recovered fast. "I know you from somewhere."

That would probably be from the back of a bus, Eva thought.

Minutes later, Kyle unlocked a private entrance sandwiched between a high-end restaurant and an award-winning café. A few seconds in a private high-speed elevator, and they stepped out into the hushed foyer of a penthouse suite.

Opening a tall bleached oak door, Kyle indicated she should precede him. A little perplexed that Kyle had brought her to his apartment, rather than a café, Eva stepped into an elegant, spare hall that opened out into a huge light space. Beech floors flowed to a wall built almost entirely of glass, with sliding doors that opened onto a patio.

The apartment was vast and overlooked the bustling Viaduct with cafés and bars and a marina filled with colorful yachts. Further out the Harbour Bridge arched across the Waitemata Harbour linking the North Shore to Auckland City. To the right the quirky suburb of Devonport with its jumble of Victorian houses was clearly visible, and beyond, in the hazy distance, the cone-shaped Rangitoto Island.

A dapper man in a suit rose from one of the long leather couches grouped around a coffee table. "Mr. Messena, Miss Atraeus."

Kyle introduced her to Ambrose Wilson, the manager of a store that was very familiar to Eva, because a branch of her family owned it. Originally Ambrosi Pearls, the Auckland branch had recently expanded into diamonds.

Wilson indicated the long, low coffee table on which were placed several black velvet display trays that glittered with an array of diamond rings.

As Eva sat down, she fought a sense of disorientation that her wedding was in two days' time.

As she stared at the gorgeous rings, words she hadn't meant to say spilled out, "Was Elise important?"

Kyle, who had shrugged out of his jacket, tossed it over the back of one of the couches and loosened off his tie. "We dated a few times. Mostly at business functions."

And they hadn't slept together, she was suddenly sure of it. Relief flooded her. She let out a breath she hadn't realized she was holding. She didn't want to feel all twisted up and jealous, but lately she seemed unable to control her moods and Elise had pushed some buttons she hadn't even known she had.

Kyle frowned. "Does it matter?"

Eva forced a smile and picked a ring at random. "Of course not."

But if Kyle had been sleeping with Elise while he had been acting as the trustee of Mario's will, surveilling her and preventing her from getting married, all bets would have been off.

The thought pulled her up sharply as she considered where it was taking her. She could only ever recall feeling like this once before, and that had been years ago when Kyle had gotten engaged to Nicola and she had been fiercely, deeply jealous. But that had been because she had been in puppy love with Kyle, and she was not in love with him now; she could not be.

A little dazed, she slipped the ring onto her finger without really seeing it.

Kyle frowned. "That one isn't right."

"How can you know that?"

"I don't spend all my time with my head buried in stocks and bonds."

She examined the ring, with its delicate bridge of three perfectly matched diamonds. It was an expensive but very conventional ring, and he was right, she didn't like it.

Kyle picked up a ring that had its own velvet tray, a classic square-cut diamond that blazed with a pure white fire. The central diamond was large but elegant and framed by tiny white diamonds that glittered and flashed. The setting was platinum, which added to the clean, classical look of the ring. "You should wear something like this. It's pure. Flawless, wouldn't you say, Wilson?"

Wilson, who had been sitting at a side table with his

laptop open, strolled over to look at the ring. "That's correct. It was originally a ten-carat diamond, but we worked with it until we achieved an utterly flawless gem."

Eva met Kyle's gaze. He lifted a brow, and she suddenly realized what he was getting at with the ring. *He knew.* He knew that she had been a virgin when they had first made love. She went hot then cold. Normally when she had a fight-or-flight reaction, her instinct was to fight. This time running would have been the preferred option.

With an effort of will, she smoothed out her expression and replaced the ring she had picked up. When she would have slipped the ring Kyle had selected onto the third finger of her left hand, he preempted her and did it himself, the brush of his fingers sending tingling heat shooting through her.

Kyle's gaze was unnervingly intent. "Do you like it?"

She was trying not to love the ring too much, but it was as perfect as Kyle's unexpected gesture in acknowledging the gift she had given him when they had made love. She cleared her throat so her voice wouldn't sound thick and husky when she spoke. "Yes, it's beautiful. Thank you."

"Good." Kyle turned his head in Wilson's direction. "We're taking the ring."

Wilson produced another box from his briefcase. "Now would be a good opportunity for you to both try on wedding rings."

Reluctantly slipping the engagement ring off, she tried the platinum band Wilson handed her for size. The band, which had been made to match the engagement ring she'd chosen, fit perfectly, so in the end the choice was a no-brainer. Returning the band to its box, she slipped the engagement ring back on her finger.

Within minutes, Wilson had packed up the cases of rings and departed. Eva had no clue what the ring cost, although she could hazard it would run into the hundreds of thousands, if not more. No money had changed hands. But, since the Messena family were bankers for The Atraeus Group and related by blood, no doubt the transaction would take place in a more relaxed way.

Kyle checked his watch. "We need to eat then I'll take you back to work."

While Kyle was taking plastic-covered plates of pre-prepared food that had been delivered by one of the restaurants downstairs out of the fridge, Eva excused herself and went in search of the bathroom. She stepped into a wide spacious hall with several bedrooms opening off it.

The hall, like the rest of the apartment, was stylish, but bare, as if Kyle had no interest in creating a home. She had noticed the lack of artwork and family photos in the sitting room, so the two framed photos gracing the wall at the far end of the hall stuck out like a sore thumb and immediately drew her.

The largest one was of a woman with long, tawny hair and a striking tan as she stood on a street in a bright, summery dress, her arms bare as she grinned and waved at the camera. Eva instantly recognized Nicola, Kyle's wife. The second frame was much smaller and showed Kyle cradling a sleeping baby, his expression intent and absorbed as he studied the small, slumbering face.

Her heart squeezed tight as she looked at the baby, and she suddenly understood why the pictures were here and not out in the sitting room, or even placed more privately in his bedroom. It was as if Kyle couldn't bear that kind of constant exposure to his loss, but neither could he bear to not have the photos, so he had placed them in the hall, an area he didn't linger.

The look on Kyle's face as he held his son briefly riveted her and, for a splintered moment, the years spun back. Her own mother hadn't coped with losing her children. And suddenly, she understood that Kyle didn't just not want more children; after what had happened, he couldn't bear to have any more.

Eva had lost her brother and sisters and, ultimately, her mother. But she could not imagine the grief of losing a child.

Feeling subtly unsettled by the window into Kyle's past, she stepped into the cool, tiled bathroom. After using the facilities, she found herself staring at her reflection and wondering how on earth she could compete with the wife Kyle had loved and chosen, and who had *died*.

On impulse, Eva took the pins out of her hair and let it fall around her shoulders, much as Nicola's had in the photo—then, feeling foolish, recoiled and repinned it.

She wasn't Nicola and never could be. Nicola had been fresh-faced, cute and athletic, while Eva was curvy and sultry and city sleek. From everything she had heard about Nicola, they were very different. There was no way she could compete. But it was also true that Kyle had never forgotten her.

Heart beating too fast, mind working overtime, Eva reviewed every conversation, the clashes and the fights, the heavy-handed surveillance, the lovemaking and the one salutary fact that couldn't be ignored. After staying away from her for ten years, Kyle had come back. And he hadn't just blended into the scenery. He had been the dominant male in her life for the past year and had systematically gotten rid of every man she had chosen.

When Eva returned from the bathroom, Kyle had set out a selection of salads, cold meats and a savory quiche on the table. She met his gaze briefly. When his scrutiny dropped to her mouth, the undisciplined tumble of thoughts coalesced into clear knowledge. Kyle had honored her condition that they did not sleep together, but at the same time he had made no bones about the fact that he still wanted her, and not just sexually. She was certain now that he wanted *her*.

Delightful warmth suffused her. Until that moment, she hadn't realized how much that would matter. But since they had made love, she felt more intimately connected with Kyle, to the point that whenever he was near she hummed with awareness.

Conscious of the weight of the ring on her finger and the flash and glitter of the pretty diamond, Eva filled her plate from a tempting selection of salads. After choosing sparkling water, she followed Kyle out onto the patio.

While she ate, Eva kept glimpsing the diamond on her finger and couldn't help the rush of pleasure that, aside from the conventional need of a ring, Kyle had been so thoughtful. Under the circumstances, she hadn't expected a ring, let alone one that was so utterly gorgeous.

Kyle caught her gaze. "I ran into Sophie and Francesca this morning."

Eva almost choked on a mouthful of sparkling water. If Sophie and Francesca had chosen lives that did not revolve around the fashion industry, they would have been CIA, FBI or some form of Special Forces covert ops, no question. As it was, within the extended Atraeus/Ambrosi/Messena family, they were a force to be reckoned with. "You ran into them or they ran you to ground?"

Kyle's mouth quirked. "We work in different parts of town, so a chance meeting isn't likely. Sophie mentioned something about a bridesmaid and a guest list."

Eva set her glass down. "Your family need to be part of the wedding—"

Kyle set his fork down. "Babe, the wedding is two days away, there's not exactly time—"

"You don't have to worry, all you need to do is turn up. All the details are taken care of."

He lifted a brow. "How many have you invited?"

Eva put her fork down. "Just close family. I know you wanted to bypass all the fuss and frills and that you probably wanted to slide the wedding through before most of your family found out, but it is still *my* wedding, probably the only wedding I'll ever have."

Kyle's head came up. "Why won't you marry again?"

She kept her expression bland. "I'm not the marrying kind. I'm just not…suited for it."

Kyle frowned, but before he could reply, his cell rang.

Eva picked at her salad while Kyle walked to one end of the patio and conducted what sounded like a business call. When he came back to the table, his expression was thoughtful, but he didn't resume the conversation.

Relieved, Eva made an effort to eat a little more. Lately, with all the turmoil, she'd been skipping meals and eating sketchily, which was bad for her stress levels. Witness the off-the-register way she kept reacting to Kyle.

When Kyle was finished, she collected their plates and carried them through to the kitchen. Carefully taking off the ring, she set it on the counter, rinsed the plates and glasses and stacked them in the dishwasher.

Kyle, who had followed her in, replaced all the food in the fridge and wiped down the counter. When she dried her hands on a kitchen towel and went to pick up the ring, he beat her to it.

Automatic tension hummed through her as he picked up her left hand and slid the ring on the third finger. Despite trying to downplay the moment, a shimmering thrill went through her at the warmth of his hands, the weight of the ring and the sheer emotion of the moment. This was what he would do on their wedding day, and they both knew it would not mean what it should. But here in the mundane surroundings of his apartment kitchen, the small act seemed laden with meaning.

Kyle's gaze connected with hers. "You're right, it is beautiful."

For a blank moment, she thought he had said, "You're beautiful." She tried for a breezy smile. "Yes. It is."

When she would have stepped back, he kept hold of her hand. If Kyle had been any other man, she would have had no problem putting an end to the tension that had sprung up. But while a cautious part of her knew she should keep things businesslike, the crazy, risk-taking part of her wanted to kiss Kyle, to pretend for just a moment that the engagement, the wedding and *he* were the real thing. Without consciously realizing she had done it, she swayed closer. "We shouldn't."

"The hell with it," Kyle murmured. "We're going to have to kiss in church, and it's not as if we haven't done it before."

The vivid memory of the passionate night they had spent together, and further back to the long-ago necking on the beach at Dolphin Bay, sent a hot flash through her that practically welded her to the spot. Seconds later, Kyle's mouth closed on hers, her arms found their way around his neck and time seemed to slow, stop.

When he finally lifted his head, Kyle studied her expression for another few seconds, as if he was contemplating kissing her again then he released her. "We need to discuss something. Why didn't you tell me you were a virgin?"

Suddenly the choice of his very private apartment for the choosing of the ring and lunch made sense, when it would have been quicker to have gone direct to the jeweler. "It's not exactly something that comes out in casual conversation."

"I thought—"

"I know what you thought." The same thing most people thought. "That I've had more men than hot dinners."

"You don't exactly put across a facade of innocence."

Eva lifted her chin. "In the modeling business, if you're tough, men leave you alone. It's a way of keeping safe."

"Now you're making me angry."

"Don't be. The strategy worked." Until Kyle.

Walking out to the sitting room, she found her bag and hooked the strap over her shoulder, ignoring the question that seemed to hang in the air.

Kyle shrugged into his jacket and adjusted his tie. "I know you're probably not going to answer, but why me, and why now?"

"You're right," she said with a trademark breezy smile, as she headed for the door. "I'm not going to answer."

Eleven

Kyle woke, uncertain what, exactly, had pulled him from yet another restless sleep. Tossing his rumpled sheets aside, he paced to the window. Opening the curtains, he looked out over the now-smooth sweep of lawn to the bay and a delicate and beautiful sunrise.

His wedding day.

Memories cascaded. Another wedding day, clear and hot and filled with family and friends. Nicola, elegant in white. She had been sweet and smart, athletic and funny. Perfect. She had fitted seamlessly into the measured pattern of his life, and when Evan had arrived, that pattern had seemed complete. Until…Germany.

His stomach tightened. Now, a marriage of convenience.

Feeling tense and unsettled, he walked through to the bathroom and flicked on the shower. The problem was, every time he looked at Eva, convenience was the last thing on his mind and the guilt that he wanted her more than he had wanted Nicola, was killing him.

Unbidden, the hours they'd spent locked together in his bed replayed, along with the uncomfortable knowledge that there had been nothing measured about his response.

And that what he had felt had somehow sneaked up on him, eclipsing the past.

His head came up at the curious clarity of the thought. Peripherally, he was aware of the sound of the shower, steam misting the bathroom mirror, the steady beat of his own heart.

He drew a breath, then another, but the tightness in his chest didn't ease. It was an odd moment to notice that Eva had done something with the bathroom. There was a new mat on the floor in a soft shade of turquoise, and brand-new thick, white towels decorated the towel rail. A large glass jar filled with soaps decorated the bathroom vanity.

The feminine, homey touches should have reminded him of Nicola, but they didn't. Somehow, they were one hundred percent, in-your-face Eva.

Moving like an automaton, he stepped beneath the stream of hot water. He considered the moment of self knowledge that had hit him like a bolt from the blue, the guilt of wanting Eva, and that what he felt was different than anything else he had ever experienced.

It occurred to him that in the years since Nicola and Evan had died, he had done his level best to lock the past away but, in doing so, he had also failed to let it go.

And in that moment he finally understood what he needed to do.

Eva stepped out on the landing just as the front door closed with a soft click.

Frowning, she walked down the stairs and glanced through the kitchen windows just in time to see Kyle dressed in jeans and a T-shirt disappear into the garage.

It was possible that he had things to do in town before the wedding, but as it was barely six o'clock, nothing would be open for hours. Dressed so casually, there was no way Kyle was going into work, either.

Feeling unsettled, not least because after the incandescent moments in Kyle's apartment, she had half expected him to follow up with a suggestion that they break the rules and sleep together, and he hadn't.

She stepped out into the hall. The Maserati cruised quietly out of the garage. On impulse, she grabbed her car keys and decided to follow Kyle. It was a little crazy and a lot desperate, but Eva couldn't help thinking something was wrong, that maybe Kyle had gotten cold feet. Given the encounter with Elise the other day, she had to wonder if Elise was the reason. It would certainly explain the cool way he had seemed to shut himself off, as if he couldn't even be bothered trying to pressure her into bed!

Eva accelerated to the end of the drive and managed to catch the taillights of the Maserati as it turned left at an intersection. Fifteen minutes of nervous tailing later, and feeling certain that Kyle would spot her, she braked outside the gates of what was unmistakably a cemetery.

Relief that she had been wrong about Elise gave way to a sick feeling in the pit of her stomach. She had chased after Kyle in a fit of jealousy and had ended up intruding on what must be a very private moment. A moment that did not include her, because Kyle was not visiting Elise or any other old girlfriend. On the day of his wedding to her, he was visiting Nicola and Evan, the wife and child he had loved and lost.

Three hours later, hours that Eva had filled by first getting her hair and nails done then sitting in the kitchen sipping tea, she finally started to get ready for her wedding.

An odd, shaky relief filled her when she heard Kyle's Maserati return. After those moments at the cemetery, her imagination had run wild and she had half expected him to walk away from the marriage.

Although, why would he? she thought flatly. After all, to Kyle it was only a marriage of convenience.

The heat of the day grew more intense and oppressive as Eva changed into the dress Sophie had designed for the simple church-and-garden wedding. A strapless gown with a tight bodice and full, romantic skirt, the dress was made even more gorgeous by the fabric, which was a soft, pale-pink-and-rose-print silk with an ivory tulle overskirt.

Unfortunately, when she came to fasten the dress, which had about thirty tiny cloth-covered buttons at the back, she could get so far and no farther.

Taking a deep breath, she checked her watch. She was running to schedule, but she hadn't considered she would need help dressing and now she was out of time to call someone to come and help her. Another one of the little details she should have thought of, but which, in the rush to get things done, had escaped her.

She glanced out the window at the smooth sweep of lawn she had made sure was mowed and manicured, to where a group of men were setting up a white tent. Walking back to the mirror, she examined her reflection. Her hair was perfect, falling loose and tousled down her back, the soft waves held with hairspray. To match the dress, she had pulled a swath back from her forehead and fastened it with a clip studded with fresh flowers.

Turning, she tried to do up a few more buttons using the mirror, but when the silk-covered buttons kept slipping from her fingers and her arms began to ache, she gave up on the job. Ideally, Jacinta should have been here to help her, but her last text had explained that she'd had car trouble and would meet her at the church.

After checking the time again, Eva stepped out into the hall and went in search of Kyle, hoping against hope that he hadn't left for the church. A door swung open. Kyle emerged from his room and she drew a breath. In a charcoal-gray morning suit, with a white shirt and a maroon silk tie that subtly echoed the deeper color of the roses on her dress, Kyle looked breathtaking.

She half expected him to say that he knew she had followed him that morning, but instead his gaze simply swept her and lingered. She found herself blushing at the soft, intense glow that seemed to make his gaze even bluer.

"I thought I wasn't supposed to see you until the church."

"Jacinta's having car trouble, so I've lost my helper." She turned and showed him the buttons she hadn't been able to reach and tried not to sound too breathless and panicky.

She had always wondered why brides got so uptight and nervous. Now she knew. There were a hundred and one things that could go wrong. Right now she was beginning to wonder if anything would go right. "If you could do the rest of the buttons?"

"No problem. I was going to break the rules and come and see you anyway."

Swallowing at the intent way he was looking at her and feeling utterly confused because she had convinced herself that the attraction he had felt for her had fizzled out, Eva led the way into the sitting room where the light was better and waited for him to fasten the last remaining buttons.

Kyle gently moved her hair aside. The backs of his

fingers brushed her skin, the small searing touch making her breath come in. She closed her eyes and worked at controlling her breathing as he systematically fastened each tiny button.

When he was finished, she opened her eyes and remembered that she was facing a mirror and that Kyle had been able to see her face the whole time. She blushed and hoped like mad that he had been too busy with the buttons to notice that she was having a minor meltdown.

He met her gaze in the mirror. "I expected you to wear white."

She stiffened a little at the reference to her virginity. "I'm over the white dress. It would have reminded me too much of my last wedding."

"The Dolphin Bay extravaganza."

"Which, luckily, paid for the dress."

He produced a case that he must have set down on a side table while he dealt with the buttons. "You should wear these today."

Still off-balance at her response to Kyle, she opened the box and went still inside when she saw a pair of diamond studs and a pendant that matched her engagement ring. "I can't accept these."

"You're an Atraeus bride and these are wedding jewels, a tradition in the Messena and Atraeus families. Mario would have given you a set if he had been alive, and Constantine will expect it." His expression softened. "Aside from that, I want you to have them."

A blush of pleasure went through her that Kyle wanted to give her a special wedding gift, even if he had tacked that bit on the end. The mention of Mario and of Constantine Atraeus, the formidable head of the Atraeus family and CEO of The Atraeus Group, made her feel even more strained. Family was important and celebrated in the Atraeus clan, even if she had never been quite sure that she had been accepted.

Kyle took the pendant from the case and unclipped it. "You don't have to wear them for me. Wear them for Mario."

"That's not fair."

"It wasn't meant to be. Turn around."

She turned and found herself once again facing the large mirror that sat over the mantel of the fireplace. As Kyle fastened the pendant, her heart turned over in her chest. Framed by the carved gilt frame of the mirror, they could have been two people who belonged in another era, another time. She touched the pretty jewel where it hung suspended in the faint hollow of her breasts. Such a small thing, yet it added an indefinable air of nurturing and belonging that made her throat close up. Like the engagement ring, she loved the pendant, not because of its value, but because of what it said about hers. "It's beautiful. Thank you."

Feeling strained and a little misty-eyed, she took the diamond studs when Kyle handed them to her. After removing the pretty pearl studs she had inserted earlier, she fastened them in place. As she did so, she couldn't help being fiercely glad that the wedding to Jeremy had not gone ahead.

Kyle had been right. For all Jeremy's plusses in terms of a convenient marriage, he had been superficial and utterly self-centered. He would never have offered to buy her even a token engagement ring, and he had expected her to pay for the wedding rings and a new wardrobe for him. "This is turning out to be an expensive wedding for you."

Kyle grinned as he checked his watch. "Lucky for me I have a bank."

* * *

Half an hour later, the limousine Eva had ordered arrived. Still feeling flustered but relieved, she attached the ivory tulle veil that slid in just above her rose clip, picked up the bouquets for herself and Jacinta that she'd ordered from her favorite florist, grabbed her handbag with her cell and strolled out to the car.

A tall dark man was leaning down, speaking to the limousine driver. He straightened and half turned and she went into shock all over again as she recognized one of her Atraeus cousins. "Constantine. What are you doing here?"

Normally, Constantine was based on Medinos, the Eastern Mediterranean island that was home to the Atraeus, Messena and Ambrosi families. Occasionally, he and his wife, Sienna, spent time in Sydney, where The Atraeus Group had an office, but he seldom came to New Zealand.

Constantine grinned. "I heard there was a wedding, so I came to give you away."

She was glad she had thought to remember her handbag because now she needed a handkerchief. Juggling the bouquets, she found one and tried to delicately blow her nose so her makeup wouldn't be spoiled. "Who told you?"

"Kyle rang a couple of days ago, so I cleared my schedule. Sienna and Amber came with me. Lucas and Carla and Zane and Lilah were in Sydney, so they hitched a ride in the jet."

Meaning that quite a large chunk of the Atraeus family, with almost no notice, had dropped what they were doing in their high-powered, fast-paced lives to be at her wedding. Eva sniffed, abruptly overwhelmed. With Mario's death, she had been feeling more and more cast adrift, and her natural instinct was to cut ties and minimize the hurt. But it seemed that the more she tried to walk away from this family, the more they found ways to tie her to them.

When she tried to thank Constantine, he gave her a quick hug around the shoulders so as not to crush the flowers then checked his watch. "Time to go." He looked around. "Kyle said there was a bridesmaid."

Eva would have crossed her fingers if she wasn't holding the flowers. "Jacinta will meet us at the church."

When they arrived there, only five minutes' drive away, the cloud cover had increased, blotting out the sun and giving the day a murky cast. Praying that the thick cloud would blow over, Eva let Constantine hand her out of the limousine. There were a few stragglers outside the church, although Eva didn't recognize any of them. She groaned when she started counting children playing around the church grounds. The Vicar had clearly forgotten to reschedule the La Leche League meeting.

A car door popped open. Jacinta waved at her, and Eva's heart sank. Jacinta wasn't wearing her pale pink bridesmaid's dress. Instead she had on a bright, summery dress, one that fairly shouted cocktails on the beach.

Jacinta looked stressed. "I'm sorry. But when I tried to fix the car, I got oil down the front of my dress and had to change."

Sienna poked her head out the church doors. When she saw Eva, she rushed over with a pretty toddler in tow. Handing Amber to Constantine, she gave Eva a hug. "You look gorgeous. Are you ready? Kyle's going nuts in there."

Eva, who seriously doubted that Kyle was going nuts, retrieved the bouquets from the backseat of the limousine. "I'm ready." She nodded at Jacinta, who gave her a relieved grin as she accepted one of the bouquets.

Sienna took Amber off Constantine's shoulder, gave Eva a last reassuring smile and strolled into the church.

Constantine held out his arm. "Ready?"

Feeling a little shaky, Eva placed her hand on Constantine's sleeve. Jacinta remembered to pull Eva's veil over her face and they were good to go.

As the "Wedding March" started and they stepped into the cloistered shadows of the church, her heart thumped hard in her chest. Someone had taken the trouble to light candles in sconces around the wall, and of course the candles on the altar were lit, the flames lending a soft glow to the wooden pews and the vaulted ceiling. There were also flowers everywhere, white-and-pink roses dripping from vases, their scent mingling with the honeyed beeswax of the candles.

Kyle, standing tall and broad-shouldered at the altar, with Gabriel keeping him company as best man, turned, and time seemed to stand still as their eyes met: his tinged with a softness she hadn't expected to see, hers brimming. A little desperately, she reminded herself that she could not afford to feel this way, and neither could Kyle.

Kyle watched as Eva walked toward him in the soft, romantic dress, which clung delicately to her narrow waist, the skirt flowing gracefully with every step. When he'd seen her standing in the hallway of his house, for a moment he'd been stunned because the dress was the exact opposite of the sophisticated gown he had expected her to wear. But in an odd way, the dress summed up the Eva he was just now beginning to know: unconventional, gorgeous and packing a punch.

Gabriel, his eldest brother, and the obvious candidate for best man, since they worked together, caught his gaze. "Are you sure you want to do this?"

Kyle glanced at Eva, noting the way she clung to Constantine's arm. She had a reputation for being tough, professional and coolly composed, but with every day that passed he was coming to understand that the image she projected was as managed as the airbrushed ads she had used to pose for. Beneath the facade the seventeen-year-old girl he had kissed on the beach was still there.

And there was the root of his problem. Somehow, he had never been able to forget Eva even though he had stayed away from her for years, even though he'd married someone else. And Mario had known it. "Yes."

Eva came to a halt beside him and Kyle met Constantine's gaze, which was as male and direct as Gabriel's challenge. Only Constantine's version carried a different message. Marrying an Atraeus was not done lightly. Mario was no longer here, which meant now he would have Constantine to contend with.

As Kyle faced Eva, he should have been painfully reminded of another wedding day, another woman, but his first wedding, as important as it had been, was now viewed through the distance of time. At some point in the past four years, he realized, time had done its work and the grief and loss, while still there, had faded.

Eva took a deep breath as Kyle folded her veil back. A little disconcerted at the steadiness of his gaze, she said her vows steadily, although when it came to the part where they would care for each other through sickness and health, she almost faltered, because that was not in the plan. Kyle placed the ring on her finger, then Gabriel handed her the ring for Kyle.

She slipped the ring on Kyle's finger and experienced a moment of fierce possessiveness. The rings symbolized the vows, commitment, belonging and the exclusiveness of the relationship.

It was not the ideal time to consider the negative implications of her veto on lovemaking, but she was abruptly aware that if she wanted the exclusivity that the rings symbolized, then sex was going to have to be part of their bargain.

Over the past couple of days, she had been brought face-to-face with the unvarnished fact that Kyle might like to have sex sometime in the next two years. She also knew from her reaction to Elise that she would not cope well if Kyle slept around.

The thought that he might have a sexual relationship with Elise or some other unnamed woman made her go still inside. That could not happen. If Kyle was going to have sex, she needed it to be with her.

In a clear voice, the priest pronounced them man and wife. Kyle took her hands and drew her close. Eva met his gaze. "We need to talk."

"Not now." Then his mouth came down on hers, and for long moments her mind went blank.

The signing of the register was a confused affair, because the adjoining room to the chapel was filled with lactating mothers and small children.

Eva signed, then Kyle. When they stepped away from the desk on which the priest had spread the papers, Sienna almost tripped over an extremely interested little person who was clutching at the fabric of her dress.

"Sorry," a pretty young mother murmured, scooping up the little girl. "She thinks you're a princess."

Eva curtsied at the little girl, who giggled. "Then she should have this." Digging in a secret little pocket at the waist of the dress, she found the little blue silk flower she had tucked in the pocket as part of the "something old, something new, something borrowed, something blue" tradition.

When the young mother tried to refuse, she insisted, pressing the silk flower into the little girl's hand. "It's just a little thing and I'd love her to have it." Words she hadn't meant to say tumbled out. "I adore kids."

The young mother picked up the child, who was already demanding the flower be sewed onto her dress. She smiled as she started back to her seat, the little girl waving happily. "Now you'll be able to have some of your own."

Blinking at the sudden wave of emotion that hit her, Eva turned back to the wedding party to find Kyle watching her with an odd expression.

"This is different," Constantine muttered, detaching a toddler from his ankle and gently turning him around so he could crawl back to his mother.

Sienna picked up a pen and signed. "No, it's good," she corrected him. "It's like a day care at a wedding. Amber can play." She moved aside for Constantine and turned to watch Amber, cute in her polka-dot dress, who was busy martialling a group of babies.

As Kyle shook hands with the priest and handed him a check, Sienna chatted about Amber until it was time to walk back into the church.

As Eva bent down to pick up her bouquet, which she'd left on a seat while she signed the register, her stomach hollowed out and her head spun. Gripping the back of the chair, she waited for the dizzy spell to pass. However, when she straightened, she was still a little off-balance.

Kyle's arm came around, steady as a rock. His expression zeroed in on hers. "Are you all right?"

"It's nothing," she muttered, although her vision was still doing weird things. "I didn't eat last night—no time. And I didn't have breakfast."

In fact, she hadn't felt like breakfast, which was unusual. Usually, she woke up ravenous.

Sienna insisted she sit down for a minute, and once she was seated, handed her a wrapped candy. "Here, chew on one of these. I know it's sugar, but they're good when you can't keep breakfast down."

Eva unwrapped the candy and popped it into her mouth. The sugar rush made her head spin, but in a good way. "How did you know I couldn't eat breakfast?"

"The same way I know I can't eat it,' Sienna said. "You're pregnant."

Twelve

Kyle's gaze flashed to hers, his expression unexpectedly grim. "Eva?"

"I can't be." She shouldn't be.

Possibilities flashed through her mind, a mixture of joy and dread, with the dread coming out on top. She wanted no part of the grief and death that had disintegrated her family. As much as she would adore to be a mother, she could not be pregnant.

A chill went through her at the thought of what a pregnancy would do to Kyle. After years grieving for his wife and child, Eva giving birth to a child that would most probably die would literally make him relive the nightmare of his past.

Eva shook her head, regretting the sharp movements almost immediately. "I am not pregnant. No way."

She smiled brightly at Sienna, and Constantine, who was regarding her in a thoughtful way that made her wonder if he could see something she couldn't. Sucking in a breath to stop the roiling in her stomach, she called on the years of acting classes she'd taken, smiled and pushed to her feet. Luckily, thanks to the sugar, she was steady.

Relief and renewed confidence steadied her even more. "See, I'm not pregnant, just hungry."

And to prove it, she would do the one thing she had been shying away from doing as a double check that the morning-after pill had worked—she would use the pregnancy test she had bought and which was still in her handbag.

It would be negative: it had to be. Relieved that she had successfully dealt with the whole idea that she might be pregnant with a child that would most likely die, and which would break both her heart and Kyle's, she forced another smile. "I feel fine now. Really."

Kyle took her arm as they strolled back into the church to a smattering of applause and began their progress down the aisle. "Do you usually skip meals?"

"Only when I'm trying to get married on a twelve-day schedule."

"Have you done a pregnancy test?"

Eva smiled at an elderly Atraeus aunt. "Not yet, but I have one…just to confirm that I'm not pregnant." They stepped out into the vestibule. A cold breeze drifted in, making her shiver.

Briskly, she decided that discussing the whole situation about sex would have to wait until they cleared up the murky area of a pregnancy. "Getting pregnant the first time we made love would be huge bad luck," she muttered. "About as likely as lightning striking the same place, twice."

Lightning flickered as they paused at the top of the church steps.

Kyle inspected the now darkened sky. "What was that you were saying about lightning?"

Her reply was drowned by a crack of thunder, and a split second later the heavens opened. Rain poured down in a heavy gray torrent, drenching the photographer Eva had commissioned. Kyle pulled Eva back into the shelter of the foyer as the photographer collapsed his tripod, flung his coat over his precious equipment and ran for his car.

Lightning flashed again, although it was sheet lightning, she consoled herself, not the jagged fork lightning that would have been an uncanny reminder of the night they had first made love.

Luckily, there was a second venue for the photographs. After twenty minutes of snapping wedding shots at the photographer's studio, Eva dismissed the limousine driver and climbed into Kyle's Maserati.

When they pulled into the driveway of the house, which was lined with guests' cars, the extent of the storm damage was clear. A heavy gust of wind had obviously lifted a corner pole of the marquee clear out of the ground, collapsing half of the tent. The caterer's van was parked near the back door entrance, which opened into the kitchen, so he had clearly made a decision to operate from the house.

Appalled, Eva didn't wait for Kyle, but popped her door open. Dragging her skirts up, she dashed through the rain, which had dropped to a soaking drizzle, making a beeline for the kitchen entrance. As she stepped into the kitchen, which thankfully was a hive of activity and awash with lovely scents, she kept repeating the mantra that in the wedding planning business disasters happened, the thing was to have a backup plan.

Once she was satisfied that the canapés and champagne were already served and that the simple summer picnic menu she'd settled on would go ahead, just inside, she walked through into the sitting room just in time to see Kyle step through the front door. There was a thin smattering of applause, which quickly died away when the guests realized that Kyle was on his own.

Taking a deep breath to control the automatic tension and outright fear that hit her every time she considered that she could be pregnant, Eva claimed Kyle's arm. Calling on all of her acting skills, she accepted congratulations, which had been cut short at the church, and when she got the chance grabbed a glass of sparkling water and nibbled on canapés.

Kyle lifted a brow at her water. "No champagne?"

Eva immediately caught his drift. If she were pregnant, she would be avoiding all alcohol. Heat flushed her cheeks, along with another sharp jab of panic. She forced a smile and tried to keep things light. "Habit. I don't usually drink at all, I don't have a head for it, and I usually only ever drink sparkling water at weddings."

They were interrupted by Constantine, who had made himself the unofficial MC. After toasts and speeches, a late lunch was served. By that time, the summer squall had passed and the sun had come out. Jacinta, who had taken control of the indoor service, opened the French doors and dried off the outdoor furniture.

Kyle and his brothers carried over the tables from the wrecked marquee, which was now steaming in the heat; guests moved out onto the patio.

Zane Atraeus, Constantine's youngest brother, styled himself the unofficial bartender, and so the day took on a shape that kept putting a lump in Eva's throat. The things she had expected to go right had crashed and burned, but the unexpected presence of her Atraeus cousins, who had come a long way *for her*, gave her something unutterably precious; for the first time she truly felt part of her own family.

When she saw Carla, the wife of Lucas, who was the third Atraeus brother, struggling to eat salad from a plate while she held her baby boy in her lap, Eva set her own plate aside and offered to hold him.

With David in her lap, contentedly chewing on a teething ring, and listening to Carla chat about the alterations she and Lucas were making to their house in Sydney, she slowly relaxed. Although, holding David, the urgent question of whether she was pregnant or not kept resurfacing. As she talked interior decorating loves and hates with Carla, she determined that she would take the pregnancy test as soon as she got a few minutes to herself.

Kyle, who was caught in a cluster of aunts who were obviously grilling him, caught her gaze, his own ironic. The small moment in the midst of the noisy gathering was oddly heartwarming. Since the tension that had arisen over the question of a pregnancy, she and Kyle had not had one private moment together.

After the cutting of the cake, which was a pretty selection of cupcakes iced with white chocolate icing and pink sugar rosebuds and arranged in tiers, with one large cake on the top tier, someone put on a classical waltz.

Kyle held out his hand. "They're playing our song."

Eva set her plate down, pleased to do so, even though the cake was delicious. The faint nausea, which had continued, was spelling a death knell to her hopes. "I hadn't planned on dancing."

He shrugged as he drew her close, his hand warm at her waist. "It's a Medinian tradition," he said, referring to the Mediterranean island from which the Messena and Atraeus families had originated.

She inhaled, catching the clean scent of his skin edged with a tantalizing whiff of a cologne that was now heart-wrenchingly familiar. Feeling suddenly absurdly fragile and as if she had to soak up scents and sights and sounds before everything came to pieces, she placed her hand on Kyle's shoulder. Their closeness shunted her back to their night together and the shattering intimacy of lying in bed with Kyle. She could still remember the way he had smelled and felt and tasted—the way he had made her feel.

She concentrated on keeping her expression smooth and serene as heat from every point of contact zinged through her. As they began to dance to a well-known waltz by Strauss, desperate to distract herself from sensations that were just a little too intense, she breathlessly asked, "What did the aunts say?"

Kyle completed a turn as they reached the edge of the patio, in the process pulling her more firmly against him. "Apparently, Mario instructed them to make sure I gave you a proper Medinian wedding."

She frowned, caught by the oddness of the phrase. "Did they assume that you would marry me?"

He hesitated long enough for her to know that she was right. "Apparently, Mario discussed it with them before he made the will."

Thankfully now, others were dancing and the noise of the music and the general buzz of conversation was enough to create the privacy she suddenly desperately needed, when it seemed that nothing about their relationship was private in the family. She knew she shouldn't be upset, but the thought that Kyle was really only marrying her because Mario had put pressure on him struck a sensitive nerve.

Everything that happened with Kyle mattered, *because she loved him*.

She went still inside as the truth she'd been avoiding for weeks finally sank in.

Not only did she love him, she had always loved him, right from the very first moment. She had even loved him when he had dumped her, which was why it had hurt so much.

She stared at a pulse beating at the side of his throat, feeling even sicker than she had when eating the cake. "But when Mario suggested you should marry me, you didn't agree."

"I promised to see you married—"

"But you would never have chosen to marry me." A couple whirled past, Zane and Lilah, utterly absorbed in one another, both wildly in love, the complete opposite of her and Kyle. "You just had to in the end, because I ran out of time."

His hold on her tightened infinitesimally. "It wasn't exactly like that and you know it."

She stopped dancing and pulled free. "Then how was it?" She felt tense and on edge, her heart pounding. She wanted to believe that Kyle felt something more for her than duty and desire, but she also knew she had to try and be objective. No burying her head in the sand.

He caught her fingers and pulled her close again. "If I hadn't wanted you for myself, I would have let you go ahead and marry one of the men you chose." He paused. "You know I want you, and after that night on the beach, I think you know how much."

She drew a breath. "What about...love?"

His gaze cooled. "What about it?"

She tilted her head and looked into Kyle's face, the blue of his eyes, his Mediterranean heritage obvious in his olive skin, the clean cut of his cheekbones and jaw. "I love you." The words were flat and declarative, but she couldn't hide what she wanted. "The question is, can you love again, after losing your wife and child?"

Can you love me?

He did a slow turn into an alcove of the room that was private. "We need to slow this down. You agreed to a legal marriage," he said quietly, "one you stipulated would be without sex. That's not exactly a recipe for love."

Eva instantly regretted trying to lever some kind of confession of love from Kyle. She hated the enigmatic expression on his face, as if he needed to conceal his emotions in case she saw what he was really feeling. She had seen that look on the faces of social workers and foster parents when she'd been passed from home to home as a kid. It was duty, minus emotion, the exact opposite of what she wanted!

She met his gaze squarely. "Can you really separate love from passion so completely?"

"Eva—"

"No, don't say it. Don't say anything." The conversation had always been risky, but she had blown it completely, because while failing to obtain any admission from Kyle, he now knew that she loved him.

Her cheeks burned at the kind of vulnerability she had spent years avoiding. "Ask a silly question…" she said a little bitterly. "People separate love from sex all the time."

Only, she never did. She had only ever slept with the one man she loved.

Turning on her heel, she left the room. As she walked, she could feel Kyle's gaze boring into her back. As soon as she stepped out into the spacious foyer, she felt better. At times their relationship had felt like a game, but it wasn't anymore; it was serious and important, because she needed Kyle to love her. This morning it had felt as if they were balanced on the brink of that possibility, but now...

Lifting her skirts, she took the stairs to the upper level. She was hot, her feet were hurting and after possibly the most embarrassing conversation of her life she needed a moment. As she stepped into the dimness of the upstairs hall, she almost walked into Constantine who was quietly strolling along with Amber dead asleep over one broad shoulder. Eva stared at the picture father and daughter made then quietly escaped into her room.

Peeling off her shoes, she sat down on the edge of her bed. Tired of coping with the dress and its long skirt, she started on the buttons and eventually managed to ease out of the layers of silk and tulle.

She changed into a light silk shift in rich summer shades of berry red, with touches of pink, purple and leaf green. Hanging the bridal gown in the closet, she slipped on a pair of comfortable sandals that left her feet mostly bare.

After checking her makeup to make sure the dampness in her eyes hadn't smudged her mascara, she spritzed herself with perfume and walked back downstairs. As she reached the last tread, the front door, which was not locked, swung quietly open and a face from the past that she hoped she would never see again stopped her in her tracks.

Sheldon Ferris, his countenance deceptively average— the boy next door grown into middle age—smiled, his gaze taking in the rich foyer, "Nice house. You've done well for yourself."

Eva's fingers tightened on the banister. "I don't know how you found me, but you need to leave now, before I ring the police."

His gaze darted to either side, checking to see if anyone was about to disturb them. "And charge me with what? Knocking on your door?"

"I know it was you who trashed my house. I haven't given the police your name yet, but if I do, by next week there could well be a warrant out for your arrest."

Fear flashed across his expression, but it was replaced almost immediately by a hard-eyed determination. "And I know why you haven't given them my name. You don't want anyone to know about your trashy background—"

"There's nothing wrong with my background."

"Then why is it such a big secret? I checked. There are plenty of stories about your modeling success, but nothing about your past. But I guess if you don't care about your gutter upbringing, you won't mind if I splash it all over the press. I can see the headline now, 'Street kid, sex symbol rises to become Atraeus heiress.'"

"You know very well I was not a street kid, or a sex—"

"Give me what I want and I won't sell the story. I'll leave you alone for good." He named a figure that was even larger than the one he had quoted before. "Pay up, and I won't tell your new husband what's wrong with you. You'll never hear from me again."

Eva sincerely doubted that. She stared at the shifty gleam in his eyes, not for the first time wondering what her mother had ever seen in him. She guessed he had been younger and handsome in a lean way; now he was a little heavier with gray at his temples and his suit had seen better days. "I'm not paying you a cent. And if you think you can threaten me with telling Kyle anything at all about my past, you can forget it. Believe me, nothing you could ever say would make any difference to our marriage."

And that was nothing more than the truth.

The sound of footsteps made Ferris shrink back onto the front porch: the fear in his expression was palpable. Eva didn't wait to see who it was, no doubt strolling from the sitting room down the hall to the bathroom. She grasped the edge of the door and looked Ferris square in the face. "Mario had information about you. Pretty sure, if I look long enough, I'll find out what it was, and when I do, I'll take it to the police."

She closed the door firmly and held her breath as the shadow of Ferris's outline seen through the frosted glass disappeared. Feeling empowered that she had faced down her ex-stepfather, who had always been something of a bully, Eva walked back upstairs to her room and found her tote bag.

Extracting her phone, she rang Auckland Central and left a message for Detective Hicks to let him know that Ferris had called at her house, demanding money. She also stated that he had been harassing her and that she was certain he was the person who had broken into her house. The next call was to the PI she had retained. He didn't pick up, either, so she left a message asking him to forward any information he had found out about Ferris to Detective Hicks.

She hung up and considered the threat Ferris had made. She knew he would carry through and go to the press, which meant she was out of time.

Her heart squeezed tight as she considered what the disclosure of her dysfunctional background and her genetic disorder would do to her relationships with her adoptive family and with Kyle. Kyle wanted her sexually, and they had shared tender moments, but he had just not had enough time to fall for her. She had hoped they would have time, but if she was pregnant, her time had run out.

When she replaced the phone in her bag, her fingers brushed the pregnancy test kit she had bought.

As much as she needed to know if she was pregnant or not, she couldn't do the test right now, because to do so was to know the truth. And if she was pregnant, she would be honor bound to tell Kyle.

In retrospect, her decision to veto sex had been a huge mistake.

She loved Kyle; she had loved him for years. It was a depressing thought, but she had to wonder if she would ever fall for anyone else, or if Kyle was it for her. If that was the case, and she was beginning to think it was, then she couldn't let him go without a fight.

She was out of time. She needed to try one last time with Kyle, no matter how exposing or hurtful it was. She needed to change the rules and exploit the one power she did hold in the hope that Kyle would, finally, fall for her.

She needed to make love to her husband on their wedding night.

Thirteen

Kyle would have followed Eva if one of the aunts hadn't buttonholed him. After frustrating minutes of listening to a genealogy that went back to some obscure coastal village in Phoenicia, now modern-day Lebanon, his younger brother, Damian, took pity on him, clapped him on the shoulder and insisted he help him with the marquee.

Snagging a couple of bottles frosted with condensation, Damian handed one to Kyle and jerked his head in the direction of the tent, which was flapping gently in the evening breeze. "Aunt Emilia and the family tree," Damian's expression took on a hunted cast. "How far back did she get? The First Crusade?"

"Not quite. You interrupted her during the Third."

"Cool. You owe me one."

Damian bypassed the marquee entirely and stopped where the edge of the lawn dropped away to the small crescent beach below. "Although, strictly speaking, I'm in your debt."

Beginning to be annoyed, because he was certain Damian was referring to his marriage, Kyle watched the sun as it sank by slow increments into the sea, casting a brassy glow across the water. "You are not in my debt."

Damian gave him an, are-you-for-real look. "You did the deed," he said mildly. "I didn't think you'd let Mario pressure you into marrying Eva."

Kyle's jaw tightened. "Don't talk about my wife like that," he said softly. He met Damian's gaze. Damian, for all his youth, was something of a hard-ass, but Kyle had lived and fought with tougher men. "Mario applied pressure on all of us, but that wasn't why I married Eva."

"I don't believe it—you're in love with her."

Kyle frowned at the conclusion Damian had reached. What he felt for Eva was deep and turbulent. When other attractions had faded, somehow the fiery sexual connection that sparked between them when they were teenagers had held. For reasons he could not fathom, Eva was different for him. But he did not think the difference was about love.

For a start, because he'd spent so many years staying away from Eva, he didn't know about large chunks of her life. Come to that, he didn't know about almost any aspect of her life until Mario had adopted her.

His lack of knowledge about Eva made him frown. He had already engaged a security firm to put together a file for him. It was too late in the day to check with them now, but he would make it his business to check on progress in the morning.

Damian finished his beer, checked his watch and indicated they should walk back to the house. "I forgot that you once had a thing for Eva. After you lost Nicola and the baby, I guess I didn't think you'd marry again."

The mention of Nicola and Evan made Kyle's chest

tighten, although, like the conversation he'd had with Eva in the car the night they'd made love, he was actually able to think of them again without reliving the horror of the explosion. Somehow, the one thing he hadn't thought would happen had: he was finally beginning to heal.

Kyle let the still-full bottle of beer dangle from his fingers. "I miss Nicola and Evan," he said flatly. He and Nicola had had a good life together. She had come from a military family and had understood the life. They had traveled together and eventually made a baby together. "But they're gone."

He frowned as the conversation referenced the thought that had not been far from his mind for a couple of weeks now, the possibility, even if it was remote, that he could be a father again despite what Eva had said.

He examined how he would feel if she was pregnant and hit the same blank wall he had lived with for years. The raw fact was he just couldn't go there again. He couldn't be a father again.

Damian strolled onto the patio. "Nice piece of real estate."

Kyle scanned the guests, although he couldn't spot Eva. "The twins told me about it."

"I didn't know Sophie and Francesca were in the market for a house."

"They weren't," he said deliberately. "Eva was."

Damian shook his head. "I don't know why I was so worried." Shaking his head, he clapped Kyle on the shoulder and strolled off to join his girlfriend. Sky was a lean blonde, with ultrashort hair and dark eyes and who could ride a stock horse almost as well as Damian.

Kyle dragged at his tie, loosening it. Damian thought he had fallen for Eva and had bought her the house as a gift. He should correct him, but there was no way he could lay bare the truth that he had used the house as leverage in order to convince Eva that she should move in with him.

The whole business had involved a ruthless streak he had not known he possessed, although it was a fact that ruthless male behavior ran in the family. Constantine had kidnapped Sienna, and Lucas had decided not to mess with a successful formula and had done the same with his wife, Carla. Kyle's oldest brother, Gabriel, had proposed a fake engagement to keep his wife Gemma in his bed, and Nick had not been much better, luring Elena to the Dolphin Bay Resort under false pretenses then cheating on a bet to get her in his bed.

Frowning when he didn't immediately see Eva, Kyle deposited the beer he hadn't bothered to drink on a table and went to find her, but instead got caught up in a flurry of goodbyes as Constantine, Lucas and Zane, all with arms full of sleepy kids, made their way to their cars. The caterer had finished packing up his equipment and had left while he'd been talking to Damian and, thankfully, so had the bevy of aunts.

Damian, his jacket slung over one shoulder, his arm wrapped securely around Sky, lifted a hand in farewell. He was followed by the twins, who grinned, kissed and hugged him, signifying that the conclusion Damian had jumped to had spread through the family like wildfire.

By the time Kyle stepped back inside, the house seemed eerily empty, except for the kitchen staff who were busily tidying up glasses and bottles in the sitting room.

Jerking his tie from his shirt, Kyle walked to the French doors and began closing the house up for the night. As he locked the last door, he checked his watch. It had been a good thirty minutes since he and Eva had argued on the dance floor.

His stomach tightened at the thought that Eva might have been upset enough to walk out. And in that moment he realized that, despite his attempts to control the way he felt about her, he hadn't succeeded. It had been evident in his knee-jerk reaction when Damian had spoken about Eva and the way he had claimed her as his wife.

It was evident in the way he felt now. Tension coursed through him at the thought that Eva might have been upset enough after their conversation to leave him, then a footfall registered and he turned to see her walking down the stairs.

A van door sliding closed then the roar of the caterer's van heading down the drive sounded.

Kyle noticed the test kit in her hands and went still inside. "What's the result?"

Eva reached the bottom of the stairs, her face oddly pale. "I haven't used it yet. I guess I'm a coward, but the plain fact is I don't want to know until tomorrow."

She slipped the tube back into its box and placed it on a hall table and walked toward him. "There's just one other thing. I've changed my mind."

She stopped close enough that she could feel the heat emanating from Kyle's skin. She ran a finger down his chest. The heady masculine scents of clean skin and the subtle spice of sandalwood made her head spin.

Kyle's hand curled over hers, holding her palm to his chest. "What about?"

Lifting up on her toes, she boldly wound one arm around his neck, leaned in close and gently bit down on one lobe. "About the clause in the agreement that prohibits sex. If anyone is going to sleep with my husband, it's going to be me."

"There's not exactly a line." When she would have drawn back, his hands closed on her hips, holding her against him. "I'll get my lawyer to strike out the clause in the morning."

"But as long as we have a verbal agreement, the new condition is in effect."

"We could shake on it," he muttered, "but I've got a better idea." Lowering his head, he finally did what she had been dying for him to do ever since the wedding ceremony; he kissed her.

Long minutes later, the world went sideways as Kyle picked her up. When he reached the top of the stairs, instead of going into her room, he continued on down the hall and into the master suite, where he set her on her feet. The sun was down now, and the room was dim with shadows. Moonlight silvered the walls and threw light over the large bed occupying the middle of the room.

Kyle cupped her face and bending, he kissed her again. "Since we have a new agreement, this is where you'll be sleeping from now on."

She tried to both kiss him and start on the buttons of his shirt. When he finally lifted his mouth, she finished the buttons. "You won't get an argument from me."

"Can I get that in writing?"

"No chance." She caught the corner of his grin, as if he liked it that she argued with him, and out of nowhere hope flared, built on the foundation of a long-ago friendship and the mystifying strength of the connection that had always sizzled between them.

"Thought so." He shrugged out of the shirt and let it drop to the floor.

Closing her arms around his neck, she lifted up against him, loving the hard-muscled planes of his body held tight against hers. She felt his fingers at the zipper of her dress. Seconds later, it drifted to the floor. Her bra followed, and she shivered at the searing heat of his skin against hers. Kyle's fingers tangled in her hair, and she found herself walked backward in the direction of the bed.

He bent his head and took one breast into his mouth, and for long moments her belly coiled tight, the room seemed to spin and there was no air.

The first few times they had made love the sensations had been intense, now they seemed even more so and the awareness of the changes to her body settled in more deeply. She could not say for sure she was pregnant, but with every fiber of her being she felt it to be so and the knowledge added a depth and poignancy to their lovemaking, because every touch, every caress could be the last.

When Kyle lifted his head, Eva ran her hands down his torso and deliberately unfastened his pants. She heard his swiftly indrawn breath, felt his tension. A split second later, he had scooped her up and deposited her on the bed. She watched as he peeled out of his trousers, but when she would have expected him to come down beside her, he remained standing and she realized he had a condom and was sheathing himself. When he climbed onto the bed beside her, she wound her arms around his neck and pulled him close.

She felt the drag of her panties as he peeled them down and obligingly shimmied a little, helping him get rid of that last barrier. She felt his gaze on her in the dimness as he came down between her legs. Loving the weight of him, she clutched at his shoulders as slowly, gently, he fitted himself to her.

His gaze connected with hers again. "Okay?"

"I'm fine." Lifting up against him, she pulled his mouth to hers and kissed him, the passion white-hot and instant as they began to move together. Long moments later, caught in a maelstrom of sensations that were almost too intense to bear, the responses peaked, jerking through her in dizzying waves. Moments later, Kyle collapsed beside her then half rolled, pulling her into a loose hold.

The room had darkened further, so that the shadows appeared inky and the moonlight by contrast threw stark, cold light over the bare floorboards and the bed.

Kyle's fingers tangled in her hair, stroking the strands, as if he loved the feel of it. Emboldened, Eva propped herself on one elbow and studied the planes and angles of his face. She cupped his jaw, enjoying the abrasive roughness of his five-o'clock shadow. "How many times can you do that?"

Kyle's head turned into her touch. He caught her hand, bringing it to his mouth. "It depends. How many times did you want?"

"Once more, at least." Gathering her courage, Eva straddled him. Since the first night together, she'd made it her business to do some in-depth research about sex and had made some fascinating discoveries in the process. "But this time I get to be on top."

Fourteen

Eva got up just as dawn touched the sky with gray. Sliding from the bed, she walked softly to her room, found her robe and belted it at her waist. Still moving quietly, she walked barefoot down to the front foyer, retrieved the test kit and took it with her into the downstairs bathroom.

After she had used the kit, she set the stick carefully down on top of the cardboard box it had come in and washed and dried her hands. There were two windows in the stick. According to the instructions, if the smaller one showed a line, that meant she had done the test correctly, if the second window also showed a line, that was a positive result.

Taking a deep breath, she checked the stick. There were two lines.

She sat down on the side of the bath, her heart pounding. She was pregnant. The morning-after pill hadn't worked.

She had known it. Her period was late, and even though so little time had passed, she felt different. Her breasts were tender and she had gone off food. Her sense of smell had become acute, so that scents that hadn't bothered her before were suddenly overpowering.

She touched her abdomen, feeling a sense of wonder that there was a baby forming inside her. In the same instant, dread struck as she wondered if, in the lottery of genetic inheritance, her baby would lose. Her twin had died at age four. Her younger brother and sister had almost made it to five.

Just long enough for her and Kyle—if he agreed they should stay together—to fall hopelessly in love with their child before having to say goodbye.

Which was why she had to leave now. Kyle had already loved and lost a baby, but at least, as tragic as his loss had been, it had happened fast and unexpectedly.

If she left now, she could go through the pregnancy and birth alone. She could choose to have the baby tested while she was pregnant, or wait until after it was born. Once she knew the result, she would contact Kyle and let him know. If the child was healthy, she would happily share custody if that's what Kyle wanted. Given that this was a Messena child, she could not imagine that he would turn his back on his child. Kyle was an honorable man; when it came to the crunch he would be a father. But she was under no illusions about how he would feel about her for forcing the issue. She did not think they would have any chance now of a real marriage.

If the child was affected, it would break *her* heart. She didn't know how she would cope alone, but she would. Her mother had never recovered from watching three of her children die, but she was determined to be stronger than that. This child was precious. She would love it for every second that it was with her and if she was very, very lucky, maybe the baby wouldn't have the disorder.

Pushing to her feet, she put the stick back in the box and dropped it in the bin then walked quietly upstairs. She had packed last night, so other than changing into a pair of jeans and a soft cotton hoodie and slipping on sneakers, she was ready to go. Although, she needed to write Kyle a note first.

Berating herself for not thinking to do that last night, she looked for pen and paper. There were pens in her tote, but the only paper was the back of an envelope. Beginning to feel a little frantic, because it was almost fully light now and she knew Kyle was an early riser, she quickly scribbled a note, explaining that she was leaving him and that she relinquished all rights to her inheritance until she was forty and that he could have the house.

The plumbing gurgled as if the upstairs shower had just been turned on, which it probably had. Adrenaline pumped. That meant Kyle was awake.

She picked up her overnight bag and checked that the hall was empty. Walking as quietly as she could, she made her way downstairs, wincing as a tread on the steps creaked under the extra weight of the bag.

She placed the note on the hall table, along with her wedding and engagement rings and paused at the door to take a last look at the house. Throat aching, tears misting her eyes, she unhooked the chain then slowly turned the big old-fashioned key in its lock so it wouldn't make a loud clunking noise and pushed the door wide.

Cool morning air swirled around her as she gently closed the door, groaning at the audible click it made. Jogging to her car, which she had parked around by the garage so that wedding guests would have plenty of room out front to park, she loaded her tote and bag.

She glanced at the kitchen windows, her heart pounding because she half expected to see Kyle, then climbed behind the wheel, started the engine and backed out. Gravel crunched beneath the tires, preternaturally loud in the early morning air. Certain Kyle must have heard, she spared a last glance for the house, but the front door was closed and windows were blank. Depressing the accelerator, she took off down the drive.

Kyle wrapped the towel around his waist when he heard the sound of Eva's car starting. Cold knowledge hit him as he strode past her room and noted that the dressing table was bare. Cursing beneath his breath, he made it down the stairs and outside in time to see the taillights of her little sports car wink as she went down the drive.

Stomach tight, he strode upstairs, found his phone and called her. When he got her answering service, he tried again just in case she was stuck in traffic and hadn't had time to pull over and answer the call. He rang a couple more times then gave up.

He found clothes, pulled on a pair of jeans and a T-shirt then tried the phone again. Jaw tightening, he retrieved the keys to his Maserati from the top of his dresser and took the stairs two at a time. It was possible Eva had gone to work, although he didn't think so. He knew for a fact that she didn't have any weddings happening for a couple of weeks, and Jacinta was running the office meantime.

He yanked the front door open then stopped when something fluttered to the floor. He picked up the envelope, which was covered with scrawled writing, as if Eva had written it in a hurry, and read then reread the words. His stomach hollowed out.

Eva had left him.

She knew that meant that she would not receive her

inheritance, but she would manage without it. Without the inheritance she couldn't buy the house, so Kyle could keep it.

Except that Kyle didn't want the house if Eva wasn't going to be in it. He had bought it for her.

Correction, he thought grimly, he had bought it for them, in order to make marriage to him more palatable for Eva.

When push had come to shove, he had been just as manipulative as Mario in trying to entice Eva back into his life.

She had left him.

His heart was pounding, and he was having trouble thinking. The last time he had felt like this had been in Germany when he had lost Nicola and Evan, but at that point there had been nothing he could do.

He had to think. Something had happened. It had to be that Eva was pregnant.

In the moment he also understood that the secrecy about Eva's past—a past he had only just begun to probe—was somehow tied in with the pregnancy. He didn't know how, but it was a fact that Eva reacted to children in a way that wasn't normal. She adored them but had seemed to recoil from the idea of being pregnant and having her own.

Setting the note back down on the hall table, he decided there was no point in driving to Eva's house or her business premises. She wouldn't be at either place, because she knew he would look there.

He did a quick search of her room. The jewelry case with the pendant and earrings was on top of a dresser. All of the dresser drawers were empty. The wedding gown and the shoes she'd worn were in the closet, but nothing else. There was no sign of the pregnancy test kit.

He checked his bedroom and the bathroom, but the small trash can was empty. Frowning, he went back downstairs and did a systematic search of the rooms. In the first-floor bathroom, he found the pregnancy test kit discarded in the trash. When he pulled out the little stick, he noted the two lines. At a guess, that meant she was pregnant. He scanned the instruction leaflet, which confirmed it.

He stared at the stick with its positive result, took a deep breath then another. He felt like he'd been kicked in the chest. Eva was pregnant with his child. He was going to be a father. Again.

The thought filled him with a crazy pastiche of emotions—delight and the cold wall he'd hit when Nicola and Evan had died; horror and grief and self-recrimination.

One other salient fact registered. He loved Eva.

Correction, he was *in love* with her, because just saying the word *love* didn't seem to encompass the intense out-of-control emotions that kept gripping him. He was in love with Eva Atraeus, and if he was honest, by varying degrees he had been in love with her since he was nineteen. But Mario's complete veto of their relationship had closed that door.

She loved him.

There was no other reason for her to run. But he had been too concerned with guarding his own emotional safety—the protective habit that had dominated the past four years—to appreciate that love.

He had fallen for Eva, but he had ruthlessly suppressed any softer feelings and focused on the sex. He had played it safe, using the surface image Eva projected as his compass north, even when he knew it was just a facade.

Now there was a child, and in that moment, he knew that nothing mattered but Eva and their child.

The specter of the past and his failure to protect his wife and child was just that, a burden of guilt he'd hung on to for too long and which hadn't changed anything. Logically, he had always known that he could never have saved them. The terrorist attack had not been predictable.

But he would not fail again. Eva was pregnant. They were going to have a child. He needed to be there for Eva and the baby—if she would let him.

That long-ago conversation with Mario suddenly made him go cold inside. He had said Eva needed protection. Protection from what? He could remember asking Mario at the time and not getting a straight answer. He had assumed Mario had meant emotional protection, but what if it was protection from something or someone else?

Suddenly the break-in at Eva's house took on an added significance. A lot of items had been strewn over the floor, but a family photo had been set on the dining room table. Annoyed with himself for missing clues that should have alerted him to the fact that Eva had a problem, he walked through to the kitchen, picked up the phone and rang Gabriel.

Gabriel picked up on the second ring, his voice gruff.

Kyle explained he was taking a few days because Eva had run out on him. "She's pregnant."

There was a small silence. "And the pregnancy's a problem?"

Put like that, Eva running out sounded like a simple reaction to an unplanned pregnancy, but Kyle knew it was a whole lot more than that. "She knows how I feel about having a child. She's gone, Gabe. She's prepared to end the marriage and let the inheritance go into trust."

"I'm listening."

Kyle filled Gabriel in on the break-in and his suspicion that someone from Eva's past was putting pressure on her, maybe with blackmail.

Kyle heard a voice in the background, Gemma, and Gabriel's voice, muffled, as if his hand was over the receiver. "I had a conversation with Mario shortly before he died. Eva had a stepfather. Apparently, he stole all of Eva's mother's possessions shortly before she died. Not content with that, he tried to blackmail Mario. There was also a medical issue, although Mario didn't go into detail about it."

The thought that Eva could be sick made Kyle frown. She had seemed perfectly healthy, but plenty of illnesses were invisible until the last stages. "I need to know more about Eva's past. I think I need to access Mario's safe deposit box."

"Meet me at the bank in thirty minutes."

Kyle hung up. Until the moment he had seen her car disappearing down the drive, he had been able to fool himself that what he and Eva had was controllable and, for want of a better word, convenient for them both.

It wasn't. Control had been an illusion. He had wanted her from the beginning. But it was more than that now. Somewhere along the way, the wanting had turned to a need that was bone deep and inexplicable.

He had always thought that love between a man and a woman came down to a romantic cocktail of sex and companionship, but what he felt for Eva was raw and primitive. She had made him see *her* and not the savvy businesswoman, and she had stunned him with her capacity to love.

She loved him.

Until that moment, he hadn't understood what it must have cost her to say those words. Still locked into the failure and guilt of his own past, the goodbyes he had said at the graves the morning of the wedding, he hadn't been able to respond.

When he hung up, he remembered the note, which was written on the back of an envelope. Walking back to the hall, he found it and reread it then turned it over. All the hairs at the base of his neck lifted when he noted that the address on the used envelope was for a PI.

Walking through to his study, he found his laptop, Googled the PI and found that Zachary Hastings specialized in locating missing persons and covering domestic situations. Certain he was close to discovering exactly what was going on in Eva's life, he checked the time. Hastings's office wouldn't be open for an hour. Frustrated, he forced himself to make coffee while he tried to phone Eva again. When she refused to pick up, he left a message, asking her to call him.

He made one more call to the young detective, Hicks, who had been investigating the break-in at Eva's house. The information that Hicks provided, that they had a suspect and that Eva had made a statement to the effect that the same suspect had been harassing her, made his jaw compress.

Hicks wouldn't provide him with the name of the person they were investigating, because all of the paperwork was under Eva's name, but Kyle was willing to bet it was the stepfather. It was just another example of how Eva, with the self-sufficient streak she had, out of necessity, acquired as a child—and which he had seen as a hard, brassy confidence—was used to managing on her own.

Gabriel was grim faced as they stepped into the sterile vault that housed their safe deposit boxes. He produced the two keys required, and Kyle opened the box, which was filled with family jewelry and documents.

Kyle found the adoption papers with Eva's birth name and those of her parents. He made a note of all three names and their birth dates. He flipped through the documents, which were mostly investment portfolios. At the bottom of the box, he found an envelope addressed to Mario. It was filled with Eva's medical reports.

"Bingo," he said softly.

Suddenly, he was beginning to have a glimmer of what Mario had meant all those years ago by Eva needing "protection." Eva had a genetic disorder. He didn't know what the implications of the disorder meant, exactly, but by the end of the day he would.

In amongst the paperwork was a psychologist's report. Apparently, after years of trying to fix the dysfunction in her family, Eva had, at age fourteen, chosen to walk away from her mother and her latest husband, a petty conman, choosing foster care and survival, instead of hopelessness.

Kyle's chest tightened as he began to see Eva's abandonment of their marriage in its correct context. She wasn't a quitter. She was strong and resolute and she had thrown everything she could into their marriage in an attempt to get him to love her back.

For Eva to leave meant she had given up on him.

If he got her back at all, it would be a miracle.

An hour later, Kyle sat down opposite Hastings in a small, neat office on the North Shore. When Hastings refused to divulge what, exactly, he was doing for Eva, Kyle applied a little judicious pressure. Eva was his wife and she had disappeared. If Hastings wanted his bill paid, then he needed to give the report to Kyle.

With the report in hand and the addresses he needed, Kyle started searching for Eva. Two weeks later, after a series of dead ends, he abandoned trying to find Eva through her past connections.

Although, he would find her, it was just a matter of time. Eva was pregnant with his child, which meant she needed medical appointments. More important, within the next few weeks, she would most probably be having tests to determine whether or not the baby was affected by the disorder. It wasn't the avenue he would have chosen to find Eva, but it was the only one she had left him.

Fifteen

Two months later, Eva dressed in a soft cotton shift dress and a light jacket, both of which were comfortable to wear, given that her waistline was gently expanding. After locking the tiny cottage she had rented in a remote coastal village miles north of Dolphin Bay, she drove to a specialist appointment in Auckland.

As she drove, she noticed the same silver sedan had been behind her ever since she had left the small village and turned onto the main highway. An odd tension gripped her at the thought that Kyle had somehow located her and was keeping tabs on her, although she almost immediately dismissed the thought. For Kyle to go to the effort of finding her and having her followed would mean that he cared, and she did not think that was the case. Besides, she was on State Highway 1, heading toward Auckland, New Zealand's largest city. Most of the traffic in front and behind would be heading toward the same destination.

Thirty minutes later, her small car was swallowed up in city traffic. A small jolt of adrenaline went through her when she noticed that there was still a silver sedan two cars behind her at a traffic light, but as she accelerated across an intersection with light-colored cars stretching in several directions, she dismissed the thought that she was being followed.

Minutes later, she parked her car and took an elevator up to the specialist clinic where she had booked her appointment. She had tossed up whether or not to have her baby tested while it was still in the womb. There was a small risk of miscarriage, but she had decided that she needed to know sooner rather than later. Regardless of the outcome, she would love this child with all her heart. If the news was bad, it would tear her to pieces, but she would cherish each day: she would cope.

As she sat in the upmarket clinic, the classical background music that was playing changed to a soft, lilting tune. It was the waltz by Strauss that she and Kyle had danced to at their wedding, just weeks ago. Nerves already stretched thin, she searched for a tissue and blew her nose, relieved when the tune finally changed to a light and airy piece by Bach.

She checked her watch. Abruptly nervous about the long wait, she got up to get a foam cup of chilled water from the dispenser in the corner of the waiting room. The sooner she had the procedure done, the sooner she could get out of Auckland and minimize the risk that she might accidentally bump into Kyle or someone else she knew.

She drank the small amount of water she'd dispensed, grimacing at the fine tremor of her hands, a sure sign of stress. The sound of the glass door at reception sliding open attracted her attention. Shock reverberated through her when she saw Kyle, dressed in a dark suit with a snowy-white shirt and blue tie, walking toward her.

She was suddenly glad that, evidently, she was the first appointment after lunch, so no one else was in the waiting area. "How did you know I'd be here?"

"I know you're pregnant and that you would need a specialist appointment, so I hired a security firm to find out where and when."

And that wasn't all. "You had me followed!"

"That, too. It took me long enough to locate you, and once I did, I wasn't taking any risks." He came to a halt beside her, and she noticed the dark circles under his eyes, as if he hadn't been sleeping, and that his hair was ruffled as if he'd dragged his fingers through it repeatedly. "I know why you ran."

She crumpled the cup and dropped it in the nearby trash can as she desperately tried to work out how much Kyle did know. She tried for a smooth, professional smile. "I am pregnant. And if you'll remember, you expressly stated that you didn't want children."

"I said a lot of things I regret, especially that. Will you hear me out?"

Tensing against the too-rapid pounding of her heart and the one thing she had not seen coming, that maybe, just maybe, Kyle wanted to try again, she sat and listened.

In terse sentences, Kyle outlined the raw details of the grief and guilt that had consumed him, almost to the point of losing her. "You know how much I wanted you. It practically drove me crazy, but I couldn't seem to change the way I was wired until I lost you." He grimaced. "Gabriel probably thinks I went crazy. It certainly felt like it."

Grimly, he outlined how he and Gabriel had accessed Mario's safe deposit box and found her medical reports. That Kyle had even rung Hicks and found that she was having Sheldon Ferris investigated for harassment. He had also found Hastings and pressured him into supplying a copy of the investigation she had commissioned into her stepfather.

"You know about the disorder."

"And that we could lose our child."

Our child. She met his gaze fiercely. "I don't understand. You didn't want a pregnancy. You can't stand the thought of having a child, let alone one that could die."

"Couldn't. Past tense."

"What does that mean, exactly?" Against all the odds, the very fact that Kyle was here, that he had gone to a great deal of trouble to find her, filled her with wild hope. Hope that she couldn't afford because she had barely survived leaving Kyle and, now that she was pregnant, she could not accept the empty, convenient marriage he preferred. And she would not, absolutely not, terminate her pregnancy.

"I followed you to the cemetery the day of the wedding. I thought—"

His gaze connected with hers for a long, tense moment. "I was saying goodbye."

Kyle pushed to his feet and did a restless circuit of the room before crouching down and taking her hands in his. "I made a mistake, about you and the baby. And about myself. I thought I couldn't heal, but I did—it just took time." In grim, rough words, he told her about his hunt for her and the research into her past that had finally made him face his own demons. "When Nicola and Evan died I blamed myself."

Despite her determination to keep as much emotional distance from Kyle as she could while he spoke, her heart broke for what he'd been through. "You couldn't protect them from a terrorist attack."

"They shouldn't have been with me in barracks. I should have made them stay in New Zealand where it was safe." He was silent for a moment. "I was waiting for them as they turned into the barracks. One minute they were there, the next there was…nothing."

Appalled, she stared at the tight clasp of his hands. "I didn't realize you had seen it." And suddenly the small scars across his stomach and arms, the nick on his cheekbone made sense. If he'd been caught by a bomb blast, he would have had multiple injuries.

She touched her abdomen. "This baby could die." In terse words she told him the grim details of her childhood.

"I know," he said simply. "But the fact that our child may have the disorder, as bad as that would be, was never the issue."

And finally she understood. Kyle had blamed himself for the deaths of his wife and child, but it hadn't ended there. Guilt had seared so deep he thought he didn't deserve love or fatherhood.

She touched his clasped hands. "I thought you were incapable of loving either me or the baby." When the reality was that Kyle was exactly what she had first thought him to be when she had fallen for him as a teenager, a strong protector who loved deeply. The way he had responded to the loss of his family only underlined that fact.

Kyle gripped her hand. "I can love you and this baby, if you'll let me."

Dimly, she heard her name being called.

When she stood up, she pulled Kyle with her. "This is my husband," she said a little shakily. "I'd like him to come into the appointment with me."

Kyle sat with her while she had the procedure. When the clinician had finished, he ascertained the time it would take to receive the test results then made some calls. Normally it took two weeks, but a hefty donation to the lab facility, and the time was reduced to forty-eight hours.

When they left the clinic, on the advice of the clinician, Kyle insisted that Eva shouldn't drive and that she needed to spend the next couple of days taking it easy.

Kyle accompanied her down in the elevator. When they reached the shadowy environs of the parking garage beneath the clinic, Eva gestured in the direction of her car. "I could move back into my place for a couple of days."

Kyle's Maserati flashed as he unlocked it. "I want you to stay at the house."

Kyle was still looking at her in an intent way that made her heart beat faster, as if he couldn't bear to let her out of his sight.

She drew a deep breath, feeling breathless and on edge but oddly, crazily confident about Kyle for the first time ever. "Why?"

He cupped her face between his hands, and she let him pull her close, loving the soft gleam in his gaze. "Because I love you. I'm in love with you. I want you back, if you'll have me."

She felt weird and a little dizzy, but the feeling was oh, so good. "Yes."

A split second later she was in his arms. The emotions that rolled through her were too powerful and intense to even think of moving; all she could do was cling to Kyle, absorb the warmth and comfort of his presence, and the stunning fact that he loved her.

She drew an impeded breath. "I love you."

A split second later, he dipped his head, and finally he kissed her.

* * *

Two days later, Kyle, who had taken time off work to be with her, took the phone call from the clinic. He handed the phone to Eva.

Fingers shaking, she listened to the result then terminated the call.

Kyle pulled her close. "What did they say? Not that it matters. For however long we have this baby, we'll love it, and if you want more we'll adopt."

Eva swallowed, hardly able to believe what she'd heard after years of fearing the worst. "They think it's all right. There's no sign of any abnormality." Then she burst into tears.

Kyle simply held her, and when she'd finished crying, he pulled her outside down to the sunlight-filled cove at the bottom of the garden.

He loosened off his hold and handed her a clean handkerchief. "I just wish you'd told me about the disorder years ago."

"I didn't know I was affected until after Mario broke us up." She shrugged. "It was after that that he took me to a specialist and I had the tests done. I think he was afraid I'd run after you." She sent him a slanting glance, "And he was right. But when I understood I was a carrier of the disease, that changed everything."

Kyle's brows jerked together. "I would never have walked away from you because of a medical issue. Mario told me to back off. He didn't say why, exactly, but he gave me the impression you came out of an abusive home, that you needed protection, not sex."

She coiled her arms around his neck, loving the feel of him so close, adjusting by slow increments to the knowledge that her future and the baby's was going to be a whole lot different than she had imagined. "Secrets are hard to let go of—they become part of you." She hesitated, but it was time to let go of her own hurt. "Did I tell you that I love you, that I've loved you for years?"

"Not today." Dipping his head, he kissed her for long, dizzying minutes.

Eva drew a deep breath as Kyle finally lifted his head. In the time they'd been talking, the sun had slid down the horizon and the shadows were lengthening. "We should go back to the house."

"First, you need to wear these." He reached into his pocket and pulled out a familiar black velvet ring box. Holding her wedding and engagement rings in one hand, he went down on one knee on the sand and slid them onto the third finger of her left hand.

In the deep, steady voice she loved so much, because it was an expression of Kyle's character, that he, himself, was steady and true, he asked her if she would be his wife for richer, for poorer, in sickness and in health.

Her throat closed up. "I will. I love you."

When he rose to his feet, she lifted up for his kiss. As they walked back to the house together, Eva knew they would have difficulties to face but, finally, she was secure in the knowledge that whatever came, they would face it together.

Epilogue

Six and a half months later, in the midst of renovations to the house they had firmly updated while keeping all of the beautiful period features, Eva put the final touches to the nursery.

Maybe it was old-fashioned to want an actual nursery opening off the master bedroom, but since she would only be pregnant this once, she had decided she would have it exactly how she wanted. The renovation and redecorating had entailed planning, hours of online browsing and multiple shopping trips, but it had been a labor of love.

Kyle, who had arrived home unexpectedly, considering that it was only two in the afternoon and he shouldn't have been home for a whole three hours, leaned against the doorjamb and surveyed the room. "It looks good." He gave her a slightly wary look as he loosened off his tie. "Is it finished?"

Eva dragged her gaze from the electric blue of Kyle's.

Months into a marriage that had been more sublime and interesting than she could have imagined, because she had never had to share her space with a man, she was even more in love with her husband.

Her husband.

The words still gave her a thrill and filled her with a glow of happiness. She and Kyle had spent time on Medinos, a honeymoon gift from Kyle so she could get in touch with her Atraeus roots and get to know her Messena relatives. She had met more family than she could poke a stick at, but the experience had been filled with laughter and healing. Most of all, she had enjoyed doing up the house with Kyle—the house that he had bought for her—working together to create a home that was a harmonious blend of them both. They still disagreed; on occasion they argued, but Eva figured that was a healthy sign.

She critically examined the white-painted armoire stacked full of diapers, baby wipes and the one hundred and one essentials a modern mother needed. "I think it's finished."

But she had thought so before then changed her mind. It was part of the nervous tension humming through her, a bit like the bridezilla thing, only with babies.

Feeling suddenly breathless, Eva walked to the window—although with her very large bump, walking was more like a waddle—and pushed it wide, letting in the early summer air. It was so hot, she was burning up. She also felt as big as a bus, probably because labor was a couple of days overdue, and if she put on any more weight she would explode.

She tried to take a deep breath, but these days breathing deeply didn't happen, no matter how much she needed the oxygen. She attempted to give Kyle a serene, in-control look. "Why are you home early?"

"I thought I should be here, just in case." He frowned. "Maybe you should sit down, or better still, lie down."

Eva tried for a smooth, professional smile. The only problem was, deep down, she was a bundle of nerves. "I was sitting down before. I hate lying down." Who could know that even lying down would be difficult when pregnant?

Abandoning his relaxed position, Kyle came to stand at the window with her. Placing his arm gently around what used to be her waist, he leaned down and kissed her. As soft and tender as it was, it was a distinctly sideways kiss. Her stomach was so large now that any approach from the front was doomed.

"Is your bag packed?"

She shifted so that she was leaning back against Kyle, his arms around her. It was the only comfortable way to hug. She let out a breath, soothed by his presence. Somehow, when Kyle arrived, all of her fretful stressing melted away. "I've been packed for weeks."

"Good, because I'm taking you to the hospital. Now."

"You knew I was having pains?"

Kyle leaned down and nuzzled her neck. "Of course I knew," he growled.

She smiled delightedly at a phenomenon that still took her by surprise, and which she had never thought would affect a macho, manly guy like Kyle. She met his gaze in his reflection in the window. "You're having them, too."

"My secretary thinks it's hilarious."

She had a moment to consider that, as crazy as it was that Kyle was experiencing some part of her discomfort, it was just another sign of how well they fit together. She had expected to feel passion and desire and all the turbulent depths of being in love with Kyle; what she hadn't expected was the warm, close companionship that had steadily grown. They weren't just husband and wife, they were best friends.

She placed her hands over his, holding his palms spread over her stomach. Almost instantly there was a sharp kick and she held her breath, riveted by Kyle's absorbed expression. "I won't tell your family…for a price."

"Too late," he muttered grimly. "Francesca knows. That's the same as saying everyone in the family knows. Constantine rang me up today to say it was okay to feel pains. Apparently it runs in the male line."

She hesitated then decided to ask. "You didn't feel them…before?"

The look he gave her was surprised. "No."

Happiness filled her at the relaxed, neutral way Kyle had answered a question about the child he had lost, because that, too, was a sign of healing. Thankfully, the guilt that had seared him finally seemed to have been exorcised.

A pain that was sharper and more prolonged than the one before made her stiffen. Concerned, Kyle helped her to the bedroom, but she refused to lie down. The bed, as comfortable and gorgeous as it was, was her nemesis. Once she got on it, she felt like a beached whale. She practically needed a crane to haul herself out.

Another pain hit her, and Kyle went white. "That's it. I'm calling the hospital. We're going now."

It wasn't a hospital so much as a private clinic because, before the police had managed to charge Ferris after they had found her laptop in his house, he had sold a story about her to a Sunday paper, and now there was a media problem. When the original story had broken, Kyle had decided it was as good a time as any to do what they had planned and fund a charity for disabled children. Unfortunately, instead of neutralizing the story, it had only seemed to whet the appetite of the media. But in a good way, and they had begun actively following her pregnancy. Now, apparently, she even had an online fan club.

Eva tried to get comfortable in Kyle's Maserati as he drove through the gates of the clinic. Thick, subtropical plantings lined the driveway, closing out any view of the rolling hill country or the sea, which she knew had to be just a couple of miles away. They weren't that far from Auckland, but the isolation seemed eerily complete.

Kyle parked in front of the double doors of a facility that, situated as it was in a mass of towering tropical growth, looked more like the set for *Jurassic Park* than a hospital, and helped her out.

Feeling grumpy and emotional the closer she got to giving birth, Eva leaned on Kyle, because she now had weird pains shooting up her legs, although secretly she loved it that he fussed around her.

An orderly strolled down a shallow ramp with a wheelchair. Eva ignored Kyle's impatience when she didn't immediately maneuver herself into the chair. Instead, she concentrated on dragging her handbag out of the Maserati, annoyed that evidently Kyle didn't think she needed this last bastion of her femininity. Grimly, she noted that given that she was now shaped like a bubble, the bag was possibly the only verifiable sign that she was female. Hugging to herself the pretty pink leather tote with cute tassels and sparkling diamanté stuck to the side, she pretended the wheelchair was invisible and shuffled right by it.

Kyle kept pace with her, his expression carefully

blank, as if he was dealing with a mental patient. "You should have gotten in the wheelchair."

"I want to walk. I need the exercise."

A series of cramps hit her. She'd had cramps on and off for weeks now. Someone had named them Braxton-Hicks cramps, because they were supposed to be practice contractions that prepared the body for labor. The Braxton-Hicks episodes had been interspersed by two sessions of false labor but, so far, no result. As far as she was concerned, Braxton-Hicks was a liar, and she had been in labor for a month. Who knew if these were finally the real thing?

She shuffled a few more steps, aiming at the front door when one of her dizzy turns hit. Head spinning, she found herself veering into the large patch of tropical bush that loomed over the front entrance. Kyle caught her before she stumbled into the weird little forest and disappeared forever. He muttered something short beneath his breath that she was pretty sure was a curse word and swung her into his arms.

"You should put me down," she muttered fretfully. "I must weigh two hundred pounds."

"No sweat." She caught the edge of a grin. "I bench press that much most days."

She thumped his shoulder, but desisted when she almost dropped her bag. It contained her makeup, a magazine, some low-sugar snacks and her phone which, judging from this place, over the next few days could be her only link to civilization.

The front doors slid open. A cool, air-conditioned current washed over her. "Okay, you can put me down now."

"No."

Feeling disempowered because he wouldn't put her down and tired of being huge and heavy and vulnerable, she muttered the direst threat she could come up with. "That's it. You just lost any say in names."

Infuriatingly, that didn't seem to make an impact. "As long as it's not Tempeste or Maverick I can live with that."

She tried not to let the fact that he didn't care about the names get to her. "Why are you so happy?"

He lowered her into the wheelchair, which the orderly had anxiously inserted into the space below her body, but by now she was in too much pain to protest. She was beginning to think that her body had finally given up practicing and was actually going to give birth.

Kyle bent down, one hand on either rest, corralling her. His face was taut, and she dimly remembered that he was experiencing at least something of these pains himself.

He kissed her, surprising her into silence. "I'm happy because after today the waiting will be over, we'll finally be a family." His mouth twisted in a wry smile. "And because we don't have to be pregnant again."

Another sharp pain hit her as he steered the wheelchair to the receptionist's desk. The woman behind it gave Kyle a concerned look, but Eva was suddenly distracted by a suspicious warmth. She couldn't be sure, but she thought her waters might have broken. Either that or she'd had another one of those annoying little accidents. "I need to go to the bathroom."

Kyle gave her a narrow-eyed look, as if he suspected her of hiding something from him. *As if.*

He had a quick-fire conversation with the receptionist then finally wheeled her in the direction of the bathrooms. She pointed at the ladies, but he totally ignored her, wheeling her into the disabled bathroom.

She sent him an outraged look when he didn't leave. "You can't come in here."

"You're in labor. You need help."

"No. I want to do this one thing by myself."

She might have been talking to a rock. With easy strength he helped her out of the chair.

When he saw the wet patch, he said another one of his cuss words. "Why didn't you say your waters had broken?"

Face flaming, she let him help her out of the wheelchair. "How would I know? It's not as if I've ever had a baby before."

Kyle's expression was grim as he helped her in the direction of the toilet.

When she was finished, Kyle helped her back into the chair and wheeled her out into the corridor. Within seconds another pain hit, this one severe enough that she was finally glad to be in the chair.

When Kyle wheeled her into her room, both a doctor and a midwife were waiting for them. She was already in active labor, and the pain was quite intense. Eva did her best to ride through the pain, silently begging for the fastest delivery possible

It was forty-five minutes.

When Kyle, who had stripped off his suit jacket and tie and rolled up his shirtsleeves so he could pace better, realized that she was in too much pain to be even remotely interested in conversation, his face went white. Stepping out into the corridor, he snapped out a curt series of commands, including a demand for pain relief.

Within seconds the room was full of people. Another lightning examination, this time by the midwife, and Eva found herself transferred to a gurney and wheeled into the delivery suite.

With walls that were a soothing aqua, and soft background music playing, it should have been an oasis of reassuring calm, but Eva barely noticed her surroundings. All of her attention was focused on what was happening at the center of her body and how much it hurt. Somehow, all of the literature she had read had managed to gloss over this part.

Kyle's arm came around her, a hard-muscled band of strength that in those moments she desperately needed. A cramp gripped her that was so prolonged and intense she couldn't breathe. Kyle's gaze locked with hers and for a precious few seconds they were bound together in commiseration.

Her fingers tightened on Kyle's as a powerful tingling surge gripped her, wiping her mind clean of anything but the sudden, irresistible urge to push. There was a brief hiatus then another series of surges, which squeezed all the breath from her lungs until, in a rush, the baby was born.

Eva floated in exhausted silence, watching, dazed, as the midwife cut the cord, wrapped her tiny baby girl in a cuddly white wrap and placed her in Kyle's hands. His gaze bright blue and indescribably soft, Kyle cradled their daughter as if she was made of fragile spun glass and placed her in Eva's arms. Wonderingly, she looked into her baby's small, perfect face, the tufts of damp hair clinging to her head, and fell in instant love. The bed depressed as Kyle sat beside her. She felt the warmth of his arm wrap protectively around her shoulders.

Reaching out a forefinger, he gently touched his daughter's cheek. One tiny starfish hand latched around his finger, and Kyle froze in place. Eva's heart squeezed tight at Kyle's careful stillness, the way his gaze was riveted on the fierce grip of his daughter, and another wave of pure love and connection hit her, this time for Kyle.

He would be a wonderful father. She had seen it in his patience with her, his quiet tolerance of the mood swings that had hit her, his absorption with all the aspects of her pregnancy. It wasn't just that her hormones had been running riot. It had been an emotional time of processing the past, of letting go and forming a new future together.

Another contraction grounded Eva with a thump. The midwife hurriedly took their daughter. A few minutes later the unutterable gift that had shaken them when cheerfully announced by her doctor months earlier, their second child, was born. It was a boy.

The midwife placed their son in Kyle's arms and Eva gave herself over to joy.

Twins: a boy and a girl. Even though twins ran on both sides of their families, it had been so much more than they had hoped for.

Kyle called his family to let them know the good news. He asked everyone to give them some space, but that was like asking waves to stop pounding on the beach.

The Messena and Atraeus families were like a force of nature. They arrived throughout the day: Luisa with Sophie and Francesca; Gabriel and Gemma; Nick and Elena; Damian and Sky; and a little later on Constantine and Sienna, who had flown in from Sydney where they were holidaying. They had all admired and held the babies and showered her with beautiful gifts and filled her room with flowers.

Later on that evening, when everyone had left, Grace Megan woke up, her cry distinctively high-pitched. Benedict Mario soon joined in, although his cry was more of a bellow.

Kyle handed her Grace then cradled Benedict. Both babies were on the small side, around six pounds each, but they were perfect.

Closing her eyes, Eva whispered a prayer of thanks.

Somehow, out of Mario's well-meant interference, she had gained everything she had wanted and more: a perfect husband and a perfect family.

* * * * *

If you liked
NEEDED: ONE CONVENIENT HUSBAND,
don't miss the other PEARL HOUSE *books*
from Fiona Brand:

Business and passion collide when two dynasties
forge ties bound by love!

A BREATHLESS BRIDE
A TANGLED AFFAIR
A PERFECT HUSBAND
THE FIANCÉE CHARADE
JUST ONE MORE NIGHT

Available now from Harlequin Desire!

If you're on Twitter, tell us what you think of
Harlequin Desire! #harlequindesire

NEVER TOO LATE
Brenda Jackson

Chapter 1

Twelve days and counting...

Pushing a lock of twisted hair that had fallen in her face behind her ear, Sienna Bradford, soon to become Sienna Davis once again, straightened her shoulders as she walked into the cabin she'd once shared with her husband— soon-to-be ex-husband.

She glanced around. Had it been just three years ago when Dane had brought her here for the first time? Three years ago when the two of them had sat there in front of the fireplace after making love, and planned their wedding? Promising that no matter what, their marriage would last forever? She took a deep breath knowing that for them, forever would end in twelve days in Judge Ratcliff's chambers.

Just thinking about it made her heart ache, but she decided it wouldn't help matters to have a pity party. What was done was done and things just hadn't worked out be-

tween her and Dane like they'd hoped. There was nothing
to do now but move on with her life. But first, according to a letter her attorney had received from Dane's attorney a few days ago, she had ten days to clear out any
and all of her belongings from the cabin, and the sooner
she got the task done, the better. Dane had agreed to let
her keep the condo if she returned full ownership of the
cabin to him. She'd had no problem with that, since he
had owned it before they married.

Sienna crossed the room, shaking off the March chill.
According to forecasters, a snowstorm was headed toward the Smoky Mountains within the next seventy-two
hours, which meant she had to hurry and pack up her
stuff and take the two-hour drive back to Charlotte. Once
she got home she intended to stay inside and curl up in
bed with a good book. Sienna smiled, thinking that a
"do nothing" weekend was just what she needed in her
too frantic life.

Her smile faded when she considered that since starting her own interior decorating business a year and a
half ago, she'd been extremely busy—and she had to
admit that was when her marital problems with Dane
had begun.

Sienna took a couple of steps toward the bedroom to
begin packing her belongings when she heard the sound
of the door opening. Turning quickly, she suddenly remembered she had forgotten to lock the door. Not smart
when she was alone in a secluded cabin high up in the
mountains, and a long way from civilization.

A scream quickly died in her throat when the person
who walked in—standing a little over six feet with dark
eyes, close-cropped black hair, chestnut coloring and a
medium build—was none other than her soon-to-be ex.

From the glare on his face, she could tell he wasn't

happy to see her. But so what? She wasn't happy to see him, either, and couldn't help wondering why he was there.

Before she could swallow the lump in her throat to ask, he crossed his arms over his broad chest, intensified his glare and said in that too sexy voice she knew so well, "I thought that was your car parked outside, Sienna. What are you doing here?"

Chapter 2

Dane wet his suddenly dry lips and immediately decided he needed a beer. Lucky for him there was a six-pack in the refrigerator from the last time he'd come to the cabin. But he didn't intend on moving an inch until Sienna told him what she was doing there.

She was nervous, he could tell. Well, that was too friggin bad. She was the one who'd filed for the divorce—he hadn't. But since she had made it clear that she wanted him out of her life, he had no problem giving her what she wanted, even if the pain was practically killing him. But she'd never know that.

"What do you think I'm doing here?" she asked smartly, reclaiming his absolute attention.

"If I knew, I wouldn't have asked," he said, giving her the same unblinking stare. And to think that at one time he actually thought she was his whole world. At some point during their marriage she had changed and transitioned into quite a character—someone he was certain he didn't know anymore.

She met his gaze for a long, level moment before placing her hands on her hips. Doing so drew his attention to her body; a body he'd seen naked countless times, a body he knew as well as his own; a body he used to ease into during the heat of passion to receive pleasure so keen and satisfying, just thinking about it made him hard.

"The reason I'm here, Dane Bradford, is because your attorney sent mine this nasty little letter demanding that I remove my stuff within ten days, and this weekend was better than next weekend. However, no thanks to you, I still had to close the shop early to beat traffic and the bad weather."

He actually smiled at the thought of her having to do that. "And I bet it almost killed you to close your shop early. Heaven forbid. You probably had to cancel a couple of appointments. Something I could never get you to do for me."

Sienna rolled her eyes. They'd had this same argument over and over again and it all boiled down to the same thing. He thought her job meant more to her than he did because of all the time she'd put into it. But what really irked her with that accusation was that before she'd even entertained the idea of quitting her job and embarking on her own business, they had talked about it and what it would mean. She would have to work her butt off and network to build a new clientele; and then there would be time spent working on decorating proposals, spending long hours in many beautiful homes of the rich and famous. And he had understood and had been supportive… at least in the beginning.

But then he began complaining that she was spending too much time away from home, away from him. Things only got worse from there, and now she was a woman who had gotten married at twenty-four and was getting divorced at twenty-seven.

"Look, Dane, it's too late to look back, reflect and complain. In twelve days you'll be free of me and I'll be free of you. I'm sure there's a woman out there who has the time and patience to—"

"Now, that's a word you don't know the meaning of, Sienna," Dane interrupted. "*Patience.* You were always in a rush, and your tolerance level for the least little thing was zero. Yeah, I know I probably annoyed the hell out of you at times. But then there were times you annoyed me, as well. Neither of us is perfect."

Sienna let out a deep breath. "I never said I was perfect, Dane."

"No, but you sure as hell acted like you thought you were, didn't you?"

Chapter 3

Dane's question struck a nerve. Considering her background, how could he assume Sienna thought she was perfect? She had come from a dysfunctional family if ever there was one. Her mother hadn't loved her father, her father loved all women except her mother, and neither seemed to love their only child. Sienna had always combated lack of love with doing the right thing, thinking that if she did, her parents would eventually love her. It didn't work. But still, she had gone through high school and college being the good girl, thinking being good would eventually pay off and earn her the love she'd always craved.

In her mind, it had when she'd met Dane, the man least likely to fall in love with her. He was the son of the millionaire Bradfords who'd made money in land development. She hadn't been his family's choice and they made sure she knew it every chance they got. Whenever she was around them, they made her feel inadequate, like she didn't measure up to their society friends, and since she didn't come from a family with a prestigious background, she wasn't good enough for their son.

She bet they wished they'd never hired the company she'd been working for to decorate their home. That's how she and Dane had met. She'd been going over fabric swatches with his mother and he'd walked in after playing a game of tennis. The rest was history. But the question of the hour was: Had she been so busy trying to succeed the past year and a half, trying to be the perfect business owner, that she eventually alienated the one person who'd mattered most to her?

"Can't answer that. Can you?" Dane said, breaking into her thoughts. "Maybe that will give you something to think about twelve days from now when you put your John Hancock on the divorce papers. Now if you'll excuse me, I have something to do," he said, walking around her toward the bedroom.

"Wait. You never said why *you're* here!"

He stopped. The intensity of his gaze sent shivers of heat through her entire body. And it didn't help matters that he was wearing jeans and a dark brown leather bomber jacket that made him look sexy as hell...as usual. "I was here a couple of weekends ago and left something behind. I came to get it."

"Were you alone?" The words rushed out before she could hold them back and immediately she wanted to smack herself. The last thing she wanted was for him to think she cared...even if she did.

He hooked his thumbs in his jeans and continued to hold her gaze. "Would it matter to you if I weren't?"

She couldn't look at him, certain he would see her lie

when she replied, "No, it wouldn't matter. What you do is none of my business."

"That's what I thought." And then he walked off toward the bedroom and closed the door.

Sienna frowned. That was another thing she didn't like about Dane. He never stayed around to finish one of their arguments. Thanks to her parents she was a pro at it, but Dane would always walk away after giving some smart parting remark that only made her that much more angry. He didn't know how to fight fair. He didn't know how to fight at all. He'd come from a family too dignified for such nonsense.

Moving toward the kitchen to see if there was anything of hers in there, Sienna happened to glance out the window.

"Oh, my God," she said, rushing over to the window. It was snowing already. No, it wasn't just snowing... There was a full-scale blizzard going on outside. What happened to the seventy-two-hour warning?

She heard Dane when he came out of the bedroom. He looked beyond her and out the window, uttering one hell of a curse word before quickly walking to the door, slinging it open and stepping outside.

In just that short period of time, everything was beginning to turn white. The last time they'd had a sudden snowstorm such as this had been a few years ago. It had been so bad the media had nicknamed it the "Beast from the East."

It seemed the Beast was back and it had turned downright spiteful. Not only was it acting ugly outside, it had placed Sienna in one hell of a predicament. She was stranded in a cabin in the Smoky Mountains with her soon-to-be ex. Things couldn't get any more bizarre than that.

Chapter 4

Moments later, when Dane stepped back into the cabin, slamming the door behind him, Sienna could tell he was so mad he could barely breathe.

"What's wrong, Dane? You being forced to cancel a date tonight?" she asked snidely. A part of her was still upset at the thought that he might have brought someone here a couple of weekends ago when they weren't officially divorced yet. The mere fact they had been separated for six months didn't count. She hadn't gone out with anyone. Indulging in a relationship with another man hadn't even crossed her mind.

He took a step toward her and she refused to back up. She was determined to maintain her ground and her composure, although the intense look in his eyes was causing crazy things to happen to her body, like it normally did whenever they were alone for any period of time. There may have been a number of things wrong with their marriage, but lack of sexual chemistry had never been one of them.

"Do you know what this means?" he asked, his voice shaking in anger.

She tilted her head to one side. "Other than I'm being forced to remain here with you for a couple of hours, no, I don't know what it means."

She saw his hands ball into fists at his sides and knew he was probably fighting the urge to strangle her. "We're not talking about hours, Sienna. Try days. Haven't you been listening to the weather reports?"

She glared at him. "Haven't you? I'm not here by myself."

"Yes, but I thought I could come up here and in ten minutes max get what I came for, and leave before the bad weather kicked in."

Sienna regretted that she hadn't been listening to the weather reports, at least not in detail. She'd known that a snowstorm was headed toward the mountains within seventy-two hours, which was why she'd thought, like Dane, that she had time to rush and get in and out before the nasty weather hit. Anything other than that, she was clueless. And what was he saying about them being up here for days instead of hours? "Yes, I did listen to the weather reports, but evidently I missed something."

He shook his head. "Evidently you missed a lot, if you think this storm is going to blow over in a couple of hours. According to forecasters, what you see isn't the worst of it, and because of that unusual cold front hovering about in the east, it may last for days."

She swallowed deeply. The thought of spending *days* alone in a cabin with Dane didn't sit well with her. "How many days are we talking about?"

"Try three or four."

She didn't want to try any at all, and as she continued to gaze into his eyes she saw a look of worry replace the anger in their dark depths. Then she knew what had him upset.

"Do we have enough food and supplies up here to hold us for three or four days?" she asked, as she began to nervously gnaw on her lower lip. The magnitude of the situation they were in was slowly dawning on her, and when he didn't answer immediately she knew they were in trouble.

Chapter 5

Dane saw the panic that suddenly lined Sienna's face. He wished he could say he didn't give a damn, but there was no way that he could. This woman would always matter to him whether she was married to him or not. From the moment he had walked into his father's study that day and their gazes had connected, he had known then, as miraculous at it had seemed, and without a word spoken between them, that he was meant to love her. And for a while he had convinced her of that, but not anymore. Evidently, at some point during their marriage, she began believing otherwise.

"Dane?"

He rubbed his hand down his face, trying to get his thoughts together. Given the situation they were in, he knew honesty was foremost. But then he'd always been honest with her, however, he doubted she could say the same for herself. "To answer your question, Sienna, I'm

not sure. Usually I keep the place well stocked of everything, but like I said earlier, I was here a couple of weekends ago, and I used a lot of the supplies then."

He refused to tell her that in a way it had been her
fault. Receiving those divorce papers had driven him
here, to wallow in self-pity, vent out his anger and drink
his pain away with a bottle of Johnny Walker Red. "I
guess we need to go check things out," he said, trying not
to get as worried as she was beginning to look.

He followed her into the kitchen, trying not to watch
the sway of her hips as she walked in front of him. The
hot, familiar sight of her in a pair of jeans and pullover
sweater had him cursing under his breath and summon-
ing up a quick remedy for the situation he found himself
in. The thought of being stranded for any amount of time
with Sienna wasn't good.

He stopped walking when she flung open the refrigerator. His six-pack of beer was still there, but little else. But
then he wasn't studying the contents of the refrigerator
as much as he was studying her. She was bent over, looking inside, but all he could think of was another time he
had walked into this kitchen and found her in that same
position, and wearing nothing more than his T-shirt that
had barely covered her bottom. It hadn't taken much for
him to go into a crazed fit of lust and quickly remove his
pajama bottoms and take her right then and there, against
the refrigerator, giving them both the orgasm of a lifetime.

"Thank goodness there are some eggs in here," she
said, intruding on his heated thoughts down memory
lane. "About half a dozen. And there's a loaf of bread that
looks edible. There's some kind of meat in the freezer,
but I'm not sure what it is, though. Looks like chicken."

She turned around and her pouty mouth tempted him
to kiss it, devour it and make her moan. He watched her

sigh deeply and then she gave him a not-so-hopeful gaze and said, "Our rations don't look good, Dane. What are we going to do?"

Chapter 6

Sienna's breath caught when the corners of Dane's mouth tilted in an irresistible smile. She'd seen the look before. She knew that smile and she also recognized that bulge pressing against his zipper. She frowned. "Don't even think it, Dane."

He leaned back against the kitchen counter. Hell, he wanted to do more than think it, he wanted to do it. But, of course, he would pretend he hadn't a clue as to what she was talking about. "What?"

Her frown deepened. "And don't act all innocent with me. I know what you were thinking."

A smile tugged deeper at Dane's lips knowing she probably did. There were some things a man couldn't hide and a rock-solid hard-on was one of them. He decided not to waste his time and hers pretending the chemistry between them was dead when they both knew it was still very much alive. "Don't ask me to apologize. It's not my fault you have so much sex appeal and my desire for you is automatic, even when we're headed for divorce court."

Dane saying the word *divorce* was a stark reminder that their life together, as they once knew it, would be over in twelve days. "Let's get back to important matters, Dane, like our survival. On a positive note, we might be able to make due if we cut back on meals, which may be hard for you with your ferocious appetite."

A wicked sounding chuckle poured from his throat. "Which one?"

Sienna swallowed as her pulse pounded in response to Dane's question. She was quickly reminded, although she wished there was some way she could forget, that her husband…or soon-to-be ex…did have two appetites. One was of a gastric nature and the other purely sexual. Thoughts of the purely sexual one had intense heat radiating all through her. Dane had devoured every inch of her body in ways she didn't even want to think about. Especially now.

She placed her hands on her hips knowing he was baiting her; really doing a hell of a lot more than that. He was stirring up feelings inside her that were making it hard for her to think straight. "Get serious, Dane."

"I am." He then came to stand in front of her. "Did you bring anything with you?"

She lifted a brow. "Anything like what?"

"Stuff to snack on. You're good for that. How you do it without gaining a pound is beyond me."

She shrugged, refusing to tell him that she used to work it off with all those in-bed, out-of-bed exercises they used to do. If he hadn't noticed then she wouldn't tell him that in six months without him in her bed, she had gained five pounds. "I might have a candy bar or two in the car."

He smiled. "That's all?"

She rolled her eyes upward. "Okay, okay, I might have a couple of bags of chips, too." She decided not to mention the three boxes of Girl Scout cookies that had been purchased that morning from a little girl standing in front of a grocery store.

"I hadn't planned to spend the night here, Dane. I had merely thought I could quickly pack things and leave."

He nodded. "Okay, I'll get the snacks from your car while I'm outside checking on some wood we'll need for the fire. The power is still on, but I can't see that lasting too much longer. I wished I would have gotten that generator fixed."

Her eyes widened in alarm. "You didn't?"

"No. So you might want to go around and gather up all the candles you can. And there should be a box of matches in one of these drawers."

"Okay."

Dane turned to leave. He then turned back around. She was nibbling on her bottom lip as he assumed she would be. "And stop worrying. We're going to make it."

When he walked out the room, Sienna leaned back against the closed refrigerator, thinking those were the exact words he'd said to her three years ago when he had asked her to marry him. Now she *was* worried because they didn't have a proved track record.

Chapter 7

After putting on the snow boots he kept at the cabin, Dane made his way out the doors, grateful for the time he wouldn't be in Sienna's presence. Being around her and still loving her like he did was hard. Even now he didn't know the reason for the divorce, other than what was noted in the papers he'd been served that day a few weeks ago. Irreconcilable differences...whatever the hell that was supposed to mean.

Sienna hadn't come to him so they could talk about any problems they were having. He had come home one day and she had moved out. He still was at a loss as to what could have been so wrong with their marriage that she could no longer see a future for them.

He would always recall that time as being the lowest point in his life. For days it was as if a part of him was missing. It had taken a while to finally pull himself together and realize she wasn't coming back no matter how many times he'd asked her to. And all it took was the receipt of that divorce petition to make him realize that Sienna wanted him out of her life, and actually believed that whatever issues kept them apart couldn't be resolved.

A little while later Dane had gathered more wood to put with the huge stack already on the back porch, glad that at least, if nothing else, they wouldn't freeze to death. The cabin was equipped with enough toiletries to hold them for at least a week, which was a good thing. And he hadn't wanted to break the news to Sienna that the meat in the freezer wasn't chicken, but deer meat that one of his clients had given him a couple of weeks ago after a hunting trip. It was good to eat, but he knew Sienna well enough to know she would have to be starving before she would consume any of it.

After rubbing his icy hands on his jeans, he stuck them into his pockets to keep them from freezing. Walking around the house, he strolled over to her car, opened the door and found the candy bars, chips and... Girl Scout cookies, he noted, lifting a brow. She hadn't mentioned them, and he saw they were her favorite kind, as well as his. He quickly recalled the first year they were married and how they shared the cookies as a midnight snack after making love. He couldn't help but smile as he remembered that night and others where they had spent time together, not just in bed but cooking in the kitchen, going to movies, concerts, parties, having picnics and just plain sitting around and talking for hours.

He suddenly realized that one of the things that had been missing from their marriage for a while was communication. When had they stopped talking? The first thought that grudgingly came to mind was when she'd begun bringing work home, letting it intrude on what had always been their time together. That's when they had begun living in separate worlds.

Dane breathed in deeply. He wanted to get back into Sienna's world and he definitely wanted her back in his. He didn't want a divorce. He wanted to keep his wife but he refused to resort to any type of manipulating, dominating or controlling tactics to do it. What he and Sienna needed was to use this weekend to keep it honest and talk openly about what had gone wrong with their marriage. They would go further by finding ways to resolve things. He still loved her and wanted to believe that deep down she still loved him.

There was only one way to find out.

Chapter 8

Sienna glanced around the room seeing all the lit candles and thinking just how romantic they made the cabin look. Taking a deep breath, she frowned in irritation, thinking that romance should be the last thing on her mind. Dane was her soon-to-be ex-husband. Whatever they once shared was over, done with, had come to a screeching end.

If only the memories weren't so strong...

She glanced out the window and saw him piling wood on the back porch. Never in her wildest dreams would she have thought her day would end up this way, with her and Dane being stranded together at the cabin—a place they always considered as their favorite getaway spot. During the first two years of their marriage, they would come here every chance they got, but in the past year she could recall them coming only once. Somewhere along the way she had stopped allowing them time even for this.

She sighed deeply, recalling how important it had been to her at the beginning of their marriage for them to make time to talk about matters of interest, whether trivial or important. They had always been attuned to each other, and Dane had always been a good listener, which to her conveyed a sign of caring and respect. But the last couple of times they had tried to talk ended up with them snapping at each other, which only built bitterness and resentment.

The lights blinked and she knew they were about to go out. She was glad that she had taken the initiative to go into the kitchen and scramble up some eggs earlier. And she was inwardly grateful that if she had to get stranded in the cabin during a snowstorm that Dane was here with her. Heaven knows she would have been a basket case had she found herself up here alone.

The lights blinked again before finally going out, but the candles provided the cabin with plenty of light. Not sure if the temperatures outside would cause the pipes to freeze, she had run plenty of water in the bathtub and kitchen sink, and filled every empty jug with water for them to drink. She'd also found batteries to put in the radio so they could keep up with any reports on the weather.

"I saw the lights go out. Are you okay?"

Sienna turned around. Dane was leaning in the doorway with his hands stuck in the pockets of his jeans. The pose made him look incredibly sexy. "Yes, I'm okay. I was able to get the candles all lit and there are plenty more."

"That's good."

"Just in case the pipes freeze and we can't use the shower, I filled the bathtub up with water so we can take a bath that way." At his raised brow she quickly added,

"Separately, of course. And I made sure I filled plenty of bottles of drinking water, too."

He nodded. "Sounds like you've been busy."

"So have you. I saw through the window when you put all that wood on the porch. It will probably come in handy."

He moved away from the door. "Yes, and with the electricity out I need to go ahead and get the fire started."

Sienna swallowed as she watched him walk toward her on his way to the fireplace, and not for the first time she thought about how remarkably handsome he was. He had that certain charisma that made women get hot all over just looking at him.

It suddenly occurred to her that he'd already got a fire started, and the way it was spreading through her was about to make her burst into flames.

Chapter 9

"You okay?" Dane asked Sienna as he walked toward her with a smile.

She nodded and cleared her throat. "Yes, why do you ask?"

"Because you're looking at me funny."

"Oh." She was vaguely aware of him walking past her to kneel in front of the fireplace. She turned and watched him, saw him move the wood around before taking a match and lighting it to start a fire. He was so good at kindling things, whether wood or the human body.

"If you like, I can make something for dinner," she decided to say, otherwise she would continue to stand there and say nothing while staring at him. It was hard trying to be normal in a rather awkward situation.

"What are our options?" he asked without looking around.

She chuckled. "An egg sandwich and tea. I made both earlier before the power went off."

He turned at that and his gaze caught hers. A smile crinkled his eyes. "Do I have a choice?"

"Not if you want to eat."

"What about those Girl Scout cookies I found in your car?"

Her eyes narrowed. "They're off-limits. You can have one of the candy bars, but the cookies are mine."

His mouth broke into a wide grin. "You have enough cookies to share, so stop being selfish."

He turned back around and she made a face at him behind his back. He was back to stoking the fire and her gaze went to his hands. Those hands used to be the givers of so much pleasure and almost ran neck and neck with his mouth...but not quite. His mouth was in a class by itself. But still, she could recall those same hands, gentle, provoking, moving all over her body; touching her everywhere and doing things to her that mere hands weren't suppose to do. However, she never had any complaints.

"Did you have any plans for tonight, Sienna?"

His words intruded into her heated thoughts. "No, why?"

"Just wondering. You thought I had a date tonight. What about you?"

She shrugged. "No. As far as I'm concerned, until we sign those final papers, I'm still legally married and wouldn't feel right going out with someone."

He turned around and locked his eyes with hers. "I know what you mean," he said. "I wouldn't feel right going out with someone else."

Heat seeped through her every pore with his words. "So you haven't been dating, either?"

"No."

There were a number of questions she wanted to ask him—how he spent his days, his nights, what his family thought of their pending divorce, what he thought of it, was he ready for it to be over for them to go their separate ways—but there was no way she could ask him any of those things. "I guess I'll go put dinner on the table."

He chuckled. "An egg sandwich and tea?"

"Yes." She turned to leave.

"Sienna?"

She turned back around. "Yes?"

"I don't like being stranded, but since I am, I'm glad it's with you."

For a moment she couldn't say anything, then she cleared her throat while backing up a couple of steps. "Ah, yeah right, same here." She backed up some more then said, "I'll go set out the food now." And then she turned and quickly left the room.

Chapter 10

Sienna glanced up when she heard Dane walk into the kitchen and smiled. "Your feast awaits you."

"Whoopee."

She laughed. "Hey, I know the feeling. I'm glad I had a nice lunch today in celebration. I took on a new client."

Dane came and joined her at the table. "Congratulations."

"Thank you."

She took a bite of her scrambled egg sandwich and a sip of her tea and then said, "It's been a long time since you seemed genuinely pleased with my accomplishments."

He glanced up after taking a sip of his own tea and stared at her for a moment. "I know and I'm sorry about that. It was hard being replaced by your work, Sienna."

She lifted her head and stared at him, met his gaze. She saw the tightness of his jaw and the firm set of his mouth. He actually believed that something could replace him with her and knowing that hit a raw and sensitive nerve. "My work never replaced you, Dane. Why did you begin feeling that way?"

Dane leaned back in his chair, tilted his head slightly. He was more than mildly surprised with her question. It was then he realized that she really didn't know. Hadn't a clue. This was the opportunity that he wanted; what he was hoping they would have. Now was the time to put aside anger, bitterness, foolish pride and whatever else was working at destroying their marriage. Now was the time for complete honesty. "You started missing dinner. Not once but twice, sometimes three times a week. Eventually, you stopped making excuses and didn't show up."

What he'd said was the truth. "But I was working and taking on new clients," she defended. "You said you would understand."

"And I did for a while and up to a point. But there is such a thing as common courtesy and mutual respect, Sienna. In the end I felt like I'd been thrown by the wayside, that you didn't care anymore about us, our love or our marriage."

She narrowed her eyes. "And why didn't you say something?"

"When? I was usually asleep when you got home and when I got up in the morning you were too sleepy to discuss anything. I invited you to lunch several times, but you couldn't fit me into your schedule."

"I had appointments."

"Yes, and I always felt because of it that your clients were more important."

"Still, I wished you would have let me know how you felt," she said, after taking another sip of tea.

"I did, several times. But you weren't listening."

She sighed deeply. "We used to know how to communicate."

"Yes, at one time we did, didn't we?" Dane said quietly. "But I'm also to blame for the failure of our marriage, our lack of communication. And then there were the problems you were having with my parents. When it came to you, I never hesitated letting my parents know when they were out of line and that I wouldn't put up with their treatment of you. But then I felt that at some point you needed to start believing that what they thought didn't matter and stand up to them.

"I honestly thought I was doing the right thing when I decided to just stay out of it and give you the chance to deal with them, to finally put them in their place. Instead, you let them erode away at your security and confidence to the point where you felt you had to prove you were worthy of them…and of me. That's what drove you to be so successful, wasn't it, Sienna? Feeling the need to prove something is what working all those long hours was all about, wasn't it?"

Chapter 11

Sienna quickly got up from the table and walked to the window. It was turning dark but she could clearly see that things hadn't let up. It was still snowing outside, worse than an hour before. She tried to concentrate on what was beyond that window and not on the question Dane had asked her.

"Sienna?"

Moments later she turned back around to face Dane, knowing he was waiting on her response. "What do you want me to say, Dane? Trust me, you don't want to get me started since you've always known how your family felt about me."

His brow furrowed sharply as he moved from the table to join her at the window, coming to stand directly in front of her. "And you've known it didn't matter one damn iota. Why would you let it continue to matter to you?"

She shook her head, tempted to bare her soul but fighting not to. "But you don't understand how important it was for your family to accept me, to love me."

Dane stepped closer, looked into eyes that were fighting to keep tears at bay.

"Wasn't my love enough, Sienna? I'd told you countless time that you didn't marry my family, you married me. I'm not proud of the fact that my parents think too highly of themselves and our family name at times, but I've constantly told you it didn't matter. Why can't you believe me?"

When she didn't say anything, he sighed deeply. "You've been around people with money before. Do all of them act like my parents?"

She thought of her best friend's family. The Steeles. "No."

"Then what should that tell you? They're my parents. I know that they aren't close to being perfect, but I love them."

"And I never wanted to do anything to make you stop loving them."

He reached up and touched her chin. "And that's what this is about, isn't it? Why you filed for a divorce. You thought that you could."

Sienna angrily wiped at a tear she couldn't contain any longer. "I didn't ever want you to have to choose."

Dane's heart ached. Evidently she didn't know just how much he loved her. "There wouldn't have been a choice to make. You're my wife. I love you. I will always love you. When we married, we became one."

He leaned down and brushed a kiss on her cheek, then several. He wanted to devour her mouth, deepen the kiss and escalate it to a level he needed it to be, but he couldn't. He wouldn't. What they needed was to talk, to communicate to try and fix whatever was wrong with their marriage. He pulled back. It was hard when he heard her soft sigh, her heated moan.

He gave in briefly to temptation and tipped her chin up, and placed a kiss on her lips. "There's plenty of hot water still left in the tank," he said softly, stroking her chin. "Go ahead and take a shower before it gets completely dark, and then I'll take one."

He continued to stroke her chin when he added, "Then what I want is for us to do something we should have done months ago, Sienna. I want us to sit down and talk. And I mean to really talk. Regain that level of communication we once had. And what I need to know more than anything is whether my love will ever be just enough for you."

Chapter 12

You're my wife. I love you. I will always love you. When we married, we became one.

Dane's words flowed through Sienna's mind as she stepped into the shower, causing a warm, fuzzy, glowing feeling to seep through her pores. Hope flared within her although she didn't want it to. She hadn't wanted to end her marriage, but when things had begun to get worse between her and Dane, she'd finally decided to take her in-laws' suggestion and get out of their son's life.

Even after three years of seeing how happy she and Dane were together, they still couldn't look beyond her past. They saw her as a nobody, a person who had married their son for his money. She had offered to sign a prenuptial before the wedding and Dane had scoffed at the suggestion, refusing to even draw one up. But still, his parents had made it known each time they saw her just how much they resented the marriage.

And no matter how many times Dane had stood up to them and had put them in their place regarding her, it would only be a matter of time before they resorted to their old ways again, though never in the presence of their son. Maybe Dane was right, and all she'd had to do was tell his parents off once and for all and that would be the end of it, but she never could find the courage to do it.

And what was so hilarious with the entire situation was that she had basically become a workaholic to become successful in her own right so they could see her as their son's equal in every way; and in trying to impress them she had alienated Dane to the point that eventually he would have gotten fed up and asked her for a divorce if she hadn't done so first.

After spending time under the spray of water, she stepped out of the shower, intent on making sure there was enough hot water left for Dane. She tried to put out of her mind the last time she had taken a shower in this stall, and how Dane had joined her in it.

Toweling off, she was grateful she still had some of her belongings at the cabin to sleep in. The last thing she needed was to parade around Dane half naked. Then they would never get any talking done.

She slipped into a T-shirt and a pair of sweatpants she found in one of the drawers. Dane wanted to talk. How could they have honest communication without getting into a discussion about his parents again? She crossed her arms, trying to ignore the chill she was beginning to feel in the air. In order to stay warm they would probably both have to sleep in front of the fireplace tonight. She didn't want to think about what the possibility of doing something like that meant.

While her cell phone still had life, she decided to let her best friend, Vanessa Steele, know that she wouldn't be returning to Charlotte tonight. Dane was right. Not everyone with money acted like his parents. The Steeles, owners of a huge manufacturing company in Charlotte, were just as wealthy as the Bradfords. But they were as down-to-earth as people could get, which proved that not everyone with a lot of money were snobs.

"Hello?"

"Van, it's Sienna."

"Sienna, I was just thinking about you. Did you make it back before that snowstorm hit?"

"No, I'm in the mountains, stranded."

"What! Do you want me to send my cousins to rescue you?"

Sienna smiled. Vanessa was talking about her four single male cousins, Chance, Sebastian, Morgan and Donovan Steele. Sienna had to admit that besides being handsome as sin, they were dependable to a fault. And of all people, she, Vanessa and Vanessa's two younger sisters, Taylor and Cheyenne, should know more than anyone since they had been notorious for getting into trouble while growing up and the brothers four had always been there to bail them out.

"No, I don't need your cousins to come and rescue me."

"What about Dane? You know how I feel about you divorcing him, Sienna. He's still legally your husband and I think I should let him know where you are and let him decide if he should—"

"Vanessa," Sienna interrupted. "You don't have to let Dane know anything. He's here, stranded with me."

Chapter 13

"How was your shower?" Dane asked Sienna when she returned to the living room a short while later.

"Great. Now it's your turn to indulge."

"Okay." Dane tried not to notice how the candlelight was flickering over Sienna's features, giving them an ethereal glow. He shoved his hands into the pockets of his jeans and for a long moment he stood there staring at her.

She lifted a brow. "What's wrong?"

"I was just thinking how incredibly beautiful you are."

Sienna breathed in deeply, trying to ignore the rush of sensations she felt from his words. "Thank you." Dane had always been a man who'd been free with his compliments. Being apart from him made her realize that was one of the things she missed, among many others.

"I'll be back in a little while," he said before leaving the room.

When he was gone, Sienna remembered the conversation she'd had with Vanessa earlier. Her best friend saw her and Dane being stranded together on the mountain as a twist of fate that Sienna should use to her advantage. Vanessa further thought that for once, Sienna should stand up to the elder Bradfords and not struggle to prove herself to them. Dane had accepted her as she was and now it was time for her to be satisfied and happy with that; after all, she wasn't married to his parents.

A part of Sienna knew that Vanessa was right, but she had been seeking love from others for so long that she hadn't been able to accept that Dane's love was all the love she needed. Before her shower he had asked if his love was enough and now she knew that it was. It was past time for her to acknowledge that fact and to let him know it.

Dane stepped out the shower and began toweling off. The bathroom carried Sienna's scent and the honeysuckle fragrance of the shower gel she enjoyed using.

Given their situation, he really should be worried what they would be faced with if the weather didn't let up in a couple of days with the little bit of food they had. But for now the thought of being stranded here with Sienna overrode all his concerns about that. In his heart, he truly believed they would manage to get through any given situation. Now he had the task of convincing her of that.

He glanced down at his left hand and studied his wedding band. Two weeks ago when he had come here for his pity party, he had taken it off in anger and thrown it in a drawer. It was only when he had returned to Charlotte that he realized he'd left it here in the cabin. At first he had shrugged it off as having no significant meaning since he would be a divorced man in a month's time anyway, but every day he'd felt that a part of him was missing.

In addition to reminding him of Sienna's absence from his life, to Dane, his ring signified their love and the vows that they had made, and a part of him refused to give that up. That's what had driven him back here this weekend—to reclaim the one element of his marriage that he refused to part with yet. Something he felt was rightfully his.

It seemed his ring wasn't the only thing that was rightfully his that he would get the chance to reclaim. More than anything, he wanted his wife back.

Chapter 14

Dane walked into the living room and stopped in his tracks. Sienna sat in front of the fireplace, cross-legged, with a tray of cookies and two glasses of wine. He knew where the cookies had come from, but where the heck had she gotten the wine?

She must have heard him because she glanced over his way and smiled. At that moment he thought she was even more breathtaking than a rose in winter. She licked her lips and immediately he thought she was even more tempting than any decadent dessert.

He cleared his throat. "Where did the wine come from?"

She licked her lips again and his body responded in an unquestionable way. He hoped the candlelight was hiding the physical effect she was having on him. "I found it in one of the kitchen cabinets. I think it's the bottle that was left when we came here to celebrate our first anniversary."

His thoughts immediately remembered that weekend. She had packed a selection of sexy lingerie and he had enjoyed removing each and every piece. She had also given him, among other things, a beautiful gold watch with the inscription engraved, *The Great Dane*. He, in turn, had given her a lover's bracelet, which was similar to a diamond tennis bracelet except that each letter of her name was etched in six of the stones.

He could still remember the single tear that had fallen from her eye when he had placed it on her wrist. That had been a special time for them, memories he would always cherish. That knowledge tightened the love that surrounded his heart. More than anything, he was determined that they settle things this weekend. He needed to make her see that he was hers and she was his. For always.

His lips creased into a smile. "I see you've decided to share the cookies, after all," he said, crossing the room to her.

She chuckled as he dropped down on the floor beside her. "Either that or run the risk of you getting up during the night and eating them all." The firelight danced through the twists on her head, highlighting the medium brown coiled strands with golden flecks. He absolutely loved the natural looking hairstyle on her.

He lifted a dark brow. "Eating them all? Three boxes?"

Her smile grew soft. "Hey, you've been known to over-indulge a few times."

He paused as heated memories consumed him, reminding him of those times he had overindulged, especially when it came to making love to her. He recalled one weekend they had gone at it almost nonstop. If she hadn't been on the pill there was no doubt in his mind that that single weekend would have made him a daddy. A very proud one, at that.

She handed him a glass of wine. "May I propose a toast?"

His smile widened. "To what?"

"The return of the Beast from the East."

He switched his gaze from her to glance out the window. Even in the dark he could see the white flecks coming down in droves. He looked back at her and cocked a brow. "We have a reason to celebrate this bad weather?"

She stared at him for a long moment, then said quietly, "Yes. The Beast is the reason we're stranded here together, and even with our low rations of food, I can't think of any other place I'd rather be...than here alone with you."

Chapter 15

Dane stared at Sienna and the intensity of that gaze made her entire body tingle, her nerve endings steam. It was pretty much like the day they'd met, when he'd walked into his father's study. She had looked up, their gazes had connected and the seriousness in the dark irises that had locked with hers had changed her life forever. She had fallen in love with him then and there.

Dane didn't say anything for a long moment as he continued to look at her, and then he lifted his wineglass and said huskily, "To the Beast...who brought me Beauty."

His words were like a sensuous stroke down her spine, and the void feeling she'd had during the past few months was slowly fading away. After the toast was made and they had both taken sips of their wine, Dane placed his glass aside and then relieved her of hers. He then slowly leaned forward and captured her mouth, tasting the wine, relishing her delectable flavor. How had she gone without this for six months? How had she survived? she wondered as his tongue devoured hers, battering deep in the heat of her mouth, licking and sucking as he wove his tongue in and out between teeth, gum and whatever wanted to serve as a barrier.

He suddenly pulled back and stared at her. A smile touched the corners of his lips. "I could keep going and going, but before we go any further we need to talk, determine what brought us to this point so it won't ever be allowed to happen again. I don't want us to ever let anything or anyone have power, more control over the vows we made three years ago."

Sienna nodded, thinking the way the firelight was dancing over his dark skin was sending an erotic frisson up her spine. "All right."

He stood. "I'll be right back."

Sienna lifted a brow, wondering where he was going and watched as he crossed the room to open the desk drawer. Like her, he had changed into a T-shirt and a pair of sweats, and as she watched him she found it difficult to breathe. He moved in such a manly way, each movement a display of fine muscles and limbs and how they worked together in graceful coordination, perfect precision. Watching him only knocked her hormones out of whack.

He returned moments later with pens and paper in hand. There was a serious expression on his face when he handed her a sheet of paper and a pen and kept the same for himself. "I want us to write down all the things we feel went wrong with our marriage, being honest to include everything. And then we'll discuss them."

She looked down at the pen and paper and then back at him. "You want me to write them down?"

"Yes, and I'll do the same."

Sienna nodded and watched as he began writing on his paper, wondering what he was jotting down. She leaned back and sighed, wondering if she could air their dirty laundry on paper, but it seemed he had no such qualms. Most couples sought the helpful guidance of marriage counselors when they found themselves in similar situations, but she hadn't given them that chance. But at this point, she would do anything to save her marriage.

So she began writing, being honest with herself and with him.

Chapter 16

Dane finished writing and glanced over at Sienna. She was still at it and had a serious expression on her features. He studied the contours of her face and his gaze dropped to her neck, and he noticed the thin gold chain. She was still wearing the heart pendant he'd given her as a wedding gift.

Deep down, Dane believed this little assignment was what they needed as the first step in repairing what had gone wrong in their marriage. Having things written down would make it easier to stay focused and not go off on a tangent. And it made one less likely to give in to the power of the mind, the wills and emotions. He wanted them to concentrate on those destructive elements and forces that had eroded away at what should have been a strong relationship.

She glanced up and met his gaze as she put the pen aside. She gave him a wry smile. "Okay, that's it."

He reached out and took her hand in his, tightening his hold on it when he saw a look of uncertainty on her face. "All right, what do you have?"

She gave him a sheepish grimace. "How about you going first?"

He gently squeezed her hand. "How about if we go together? I'll start off and then we'll alternate."

She nodded. "What if we have the same ones?"

"That will be okay. We'll talk about all of them." He picked up his piece of paper.

"First on my list is communication."

Sienna smiled ruefully. "It's first on mine, too. And I agree that we need to talk more, without arguing, not that you argued. I think you would hold stuff in when I made you upset instead of getting it out and speaking your mind."

Dane stared at her for a moment, then a smile touched his lips. "You're right, you know. I always had to plug in the last word and I did it because I knew it would piss you off."

"Well, stop doing it."

He grinned. "Okay. The next time I'll hang around for us to talk through things. But then you're going to have to make sure that you're available when we need to talk. You can't let anything, not even your job, get in the way of us communicating."

"Okay, I agree."

"Now, what's next on your list?" he asked.

She looked up at him and smiled. "Patience. I know you said that I don't have patience, but neither do you. But you used to."

Dane shook his head. "Yeah, I lost my patience when you did. I thought to myself, why should I be patient with you when you weren't doing the same with me? Sometimes I think you thought I enjoyed knowing you had a bad day or didn't make a sale, and that wasn't it at all. At some point what was suddenly important to you wasn't important to me anymore."

"And because of it, we both became detached," Sienna said softly.

"Yes, we did." He reached out and lifted her chin. "I promise to do a better job of being patient, Sienna."

"So will I, Dane."

They alternated, going down the list. They had a number of the same things on both lists and they discussed everything in detail, acknowledging their faults and what they could have done to make things better. They also discussed what they would do in the future to strengthen their marriage.

"That's all I have on my list," Dane said a while later. "Do you have anything else?"

Sienna's finger glided over her list. For a short while she thought about pretending she didn't have anything else, but they had agreed to be completely honest. They had definitely done so when they had discussed her spending more time at work than at home.

"So what's the last thing on your list, Sienna? What do you see as one of the things that went wrong with our marriage?"

She lifted her chin and met his gaze and said, "My inability to stand up to your parents."

He looked at her with deep, dark eyes. "Okay, then. Let's talk about that."

Chapter 17

Dane waited patiently for Sienna to begin talking and gently rubbed the backside of her hand while doing so. He'd known the issue of his parents had always been a challenge to her. Over the years, he had tried to make her see that how the elder Bradfords felt didn't matter. What he failed to realize, accept and understand was that it *did* matter…to her.

She had grown up in a family without love for so long that when they married, she not only sought his love, but that of his family. Being accepted meant a lot to her, and her expectations of the Bradfords, given how they operated and their family history, were too high.

They weren't a close-knit bunch, never had been and never would be. His parents had allowed their own parents to decide their future, including who they married. When they had come of age, arranged marriages were the norm within the Bradfords' circle. His father had once confided to him one night after indulging in too many drinks that his mother had not been his choice for a wife. That hadn't surprised Dane, nor had it bothered him, since he would bet that his father probably hadn't been his mother's choice of a husband, either.

"I don't want to rehash the past, Dane," Sienna finally said softly, looking at the blaze in the fireplace instead of at him. "But something you said earlier tonight has made me think about a lot of things. You love your parents, but you've never hesitated in letting them know when you felt they were wrong, nor have you put up with their crap when it came to me."

She switched her gaze from the fire to him. "The problem is that *I* put up with their crap when it came to me. And you were right. I thought I had to actually prove something to them, show them I was worthy of you and your love. And I've spent the better part of a year and a half doing that and all it did was bring me closer and closer to losing you. I'm sure they've been walking around with big smiles on their faces since you got the divorce petition. But I refuse to let them be happy at my expense and my own heartbreak."

She scooted closer to Dane and splayed her hands against his chest. "It's time I became more assertive with your parents, Dane. Because it's not about them—it's about us. I refuse to let them make me feel unworthy any longer, because I am worthy to be loved by you. I don't have anything to prove. They either accept me as I am or not at all. The only person who matters anymore is you."

With his gaze holding hers, Dane lifted one of her hands off his chest and brought it to his lips, and placed a kiss on the palm. "I'm glad you've finally come to re-alize that, Sienna. And I wholeheartedly understand and agree. I was made to love you, and if my parents never accept that then it's their loss, not ours."

Tears constricted Sienna's throat and she swallowed deeply before she could find her voice to say, "I love you, Dane. I don't want the divorce. I never did. I want to belong to you and I want you to belong to me. I just want to make you happy."

"And I love you, too, Sienna, and I don't want the divorce, either. My life will be nothing without you being a part of it. I love you so much and I've missed you."

And with his heart pounding hard in his chest, he leaned over and captured her lips, intent on showing her just what he meant.

Chapter 18

This is homecoming, Sienna thought as she was quickly consumed by the hungry onslaught of Dane's kiss. All the hurt and anger she'd felt for six months was being replaced by passion of the most heated kind. All she could think about was the desire she was feeling being back in the arms of the man she loved and who loved her.

This was the type of communication she'd always loved, where she could share her thoughts, feelings and desires with Dane without uttering a single word. It was where their deepest emotions and what was in their inner hearts spoke for them, expressing things so eloquently and not leaving any room for misunderstandings.

He pulled back slightly, his lips hovering within inches of hers. He reached out and caressed her cheek, and as if she needed his taste again, her lips automatically parted. A slow, sensual acknowledgement of understanding tilted the corners of his mouth into a smile. Then he leaned closer and kissed her again, longer and harder, and the only thing she could do was to wrap her arms around him and silently thank God for reuniting her with this very special man.

Dane was hungry for the taste of his wife and at that moment, as his heart continued to pound relentlessly in his chest, he knew he had to make love to her, to show her in every way what she meant to him, had always meant to him and would always mean to him.

He pulled back slightly and the moisture that was left on her lips made his stomach clench. He leaned forward and licked them dry, or tried to, but her scent was driving him to do more. "Please let me make love to you, Sienna," he whispered, leaning down and resting his forehead against hers.

She leaned back and cupped his chin with her hand. "Oh, yes. I want you to make love to me, Dane. I've missed being with you so much I ache."

"Oh, baby, I love you." He pulled her closer, murmured the words in her twisted locks, kissed her cheek, her temple, her lips, and he cupped her buttocks, practically lifting her off the floor in the process. His breath came out harsh, ragged, as the chemistry between them sizzled. There was only one way to drench their fire.

He stretched out with her in front of the fireplace as he began removing her clothes and then his. Moments later, the blaze from the fire was a flickering light across their naked skin. And then he began kissing her all over, leaving no part of her untouched, determined to quench his hunger and his desire. He had missed the taste of her and was determined to be reacquainted in every way he could think of.

"Dane…"

Her tortured moan ignited the passion within him and

he leaned forward to position his body over hers, letting
his throbbing erection come to rest between her thighs,
gently touching the entrance of her moist heat. He lifted
his head to look down at her, wanting to see her expression the exact moment their bodies joined again.

And at that moment she forgot everything—the Beast from the East, their limited supply of food and the fact they were stranded together in a cabin with barely enough heat. The only thing that registered in her mind was that they were together and expressing their love in a way that literally touched her soul.

He continued to stroke her, in and out, and with each powerful thrust into her body she moaned out his name and told him of her love. She was like a bow whose strings were being stretched to the limit each and every time he drove into her, and she met his thrusts with her own eager ones.

And then she felt it, the strength like a volcano erupting as he continued to stroke her to oblivion. Her body splintered into a thousand pieces as an orgasm ripped through her, almost snatching her breath away. And when she felt him buck, tighten his hold on her hips and thrust into her deeper, she knew that same powerful sensation had taken hold of him, as well.

"Sienna!"

He screamed her name and growled a couple of words that were incoherent to her ears. She tightened her arms around his neck, needing to be as close to him as she could get. She knew in her heart at that moment that things were going to be fine. She and Dane had proved that when it came to the power of love, it was never too late.

Sienna awoke the following morning naked, in front of the fireplace and cuddled in her husband's arms with a blanket covering them. After yawning, she raised her chin and glanced over at him and met his gaze head-on. The intensity in the dark eyes staring back at her shot heat through all parts of her body. She couldn't help but

Chapter 19

Sienna stared into Dane's eyes, the heat and passion she saw in them making her shiver. The love she recognized made her heart pound, and the desire she felt for him sent surges and surges of sensations through every part of her body, especially the area between her legs, making her thighs quiver.

"You're my everything, Sienna," he whispered as he began easing inside of her. His gaze was locked with hers as his voice came out in a husky tone. "I need you like I need air to breathe, water for thirst and food for nourishment. Oh, baby, my life has been so empty since you've been gone. I love and need you."

His words touched her and when he was embedded inside of her to the hilt, she arched her back, needing and wanting even more of him. She gripped his shoulders with her fingers as liquid fire seemed to flow to all parts of her body.

recall last night and how they had tried making up for all the time they had been apart.

"It's gone," Dane said softly, pulling her closer into his arms.

She lifted a brow. "What's gone?"

"The Beast."

She tilted her head to glance out the window and he was right. Although snow was still falling, it wasn't the violent blizzard that had been unleashed the day before. It was as if the weather had served the purpose it had come for and had made its exit. She smiled. Evidently, someone up there knew she and Dane's relationship was meant to be saved and had stepped in to salvage it.

She was about to say something when suddenly there was a loud pounding at the door. She and Dane looked at each other, wondering who would be paying them a visit to the cabin at this hour and in this weather.

Chapter 20

Sienna, like Dane, had quickly gotten dressed and was now staring at the four men who were standing in the doorway...those handsome Steele brothers. She smiled, shaking her head. Vanessa had evidently called her cousins to come rescue her, anyway.

"Vanessa called us," Chance Steele, the oldest of the pack, said by way of explanation. "It just so happened that we were only a couple of miles down the road at our own cabin." A smile touched his lips. "She was concerned that the two of you were here starving to death and asked us to share some of our rations."

"Thanks, guys," Dane said, gladly accepting the box Sebastian Steele was handing him. "Come on in. And although we've had plenty of heat to keep us warm, I have to admit our food supply was kind of low."

As soon as the four entered, all eyes went to Sienna. Although the brothers knew Dane because their families sometimes ran in the same social circles, as well as the fact that Dane and Donovan Steele had graduated from high school the same year, she knew their main concern was for her. She had been their cousin Vanessa's best friend for years, and as a result they had sort of adopted her as their little cousin, as well.

"You okay?" Morgan Steele asked her, although Sienna knew she had to look fine; probably like a woman who'd been made love to all night, and she wasn't ashamed of that fact. After all, Dane *was* her husband. But the Steeles knew about her pending divorce, so she decided to end their worries.

She smiled and moved closer to Dane. He automatically wrapped his arms around her shoulders and brought her closer to his side. "Yes, I'm wonderful," she said, breaking the subtle tension she felt in the room. "Dane and I have decided we don't want a divorce and intend to stay together and make our marriage work."

The relieved smiles on the faces of the four men were priceless. "That's wonderful. We're happy for you," Donovan Steele said, grinning.

"We apologize if we interrupted anything, but you know Vanessa," Chance said, smiling. "She wouldn't let up. We would have come sooner but the bad weather kept us away."

"Your timing was perfect," Dane said, grinning. "We appreciate you even coming out now. I'm sure the roads weren't their best."

"No, but my new truck managed just fine," Sebastian said proudly. "Besides, we're going fishing later. We would invite you to join us, Dane, but I'm sure you can think of other ways you'd prefer to spend your time."

Dane smiled as he glanced down and met Sienna's gaze. "Oh, yeah, I can definitely think of a few."

The power had been restored and a couple of hours later, after eating a hefty breakfast of pancakes, sausage, grits and eggs, and drinking what Dane had to admit was the best coffee he'd had in a long time, Dane and Sienna were wrapped in each other's arms in the king-size bed. Sensations flowed through her just thinking about how they had ached and hungered for each other, and the fierceness of their lovemaking to fulfill that need and greed.

"Now will you tell me what brought you to the cabin?" Sienna asked, turning in Dane's arms and meeting his gaze.

"My wedding band." He then told her why he'd come to the cabin two weeks ago and how he'd left the ring behind. "It was as if without that ring on my finger, my connection to you was gone. I had to have it back so I came here for it."

Sienna nodded, understanding completely. That was one of the reasons she hadn't removed hers. Reaching out she cupped his stubble jaw in her hand and then leaned over and kissed him softly. "Together forever, Mr. Bradford."

Dane smiled. "Yes, Mrs. Bradford, together forever. We've proved that when it comes to true love, it's never too late."

* * * * *

"You're a rich, powerful, unmarried businessman. You're better suited to run a corporation than to change a diaper. I'm willing to bet you don't have the first clue of how to care for an infant, much less the time."

Luca just shook his head and sat forward in his seat. "You know very little about me, *tesorino*, you've said so yourself, so don't presume anything about me."

Claire narrowed her gaze at him. She definitely didn't like him pushing her. And he was pushing her. Partially because he liked to see the fire in her eyes and the flush of her skin, and partially because it was necessary to get through to her.

Neither of them had asked for this to happen to them, but she needed to learn she wasn't in charge. They had to cooperate if this awkward situation was going to improve. He'd started off nice, politely requesting to see Eva, and he'd been flatly ignored. As each request was met with silence, he'd escalated the pressure. That's how they'd ended up here today. If she pushed him any further, he would start playing hardball. He didn't want to, but he would crush her like his restaurants' competitors.

"We can work together and play nice, or my lawyer here can make things very difficult for you. As he said, it's your choice."

"What are you suggesting, Mr. Moretti?" her lawyer asked.

"I'm suggesting we both take a little time away from our jobs and spend it together."

Don't miss
THE CEO'S UNEXPECTED CHILD
by Andrea Laurence, available March 2016 wherever
Harlequin® Desire books and ebooks are sold.

www.Harlequin.com

COMING NEXT MONTH FROM

HARLEQUIN®
Desire

Available March 1, 2016

#2431 THE CEO'S UNEXPECTED CHILD
Billionaires and Babies • by Andrea Laurence
When a fertility clinic makes a mistake, a recent widow discovers her infant daughter doesn't belong to her late husband, but to a billionaire set on claiming his new family...by any means.

#2432 THE SEAL'S SECRET HEIRS
Texas Cattleman's Club: Lies and Lullabies
by Kat Cantrell
A former Navy SEAL comes home to his greatest challenge yet—surprise fatherhood of secret twins—only to discover his high school sweetheart is his children's social worker. Will the first-time father get a second shot at real love?

#2433 SNOWBOUND WITH THE BOSS
Pregnant by the Boss • by Maureen Child
When gaming tycoon Sean Ryan is stranded with irascible, irresistible contractor Kate Wells, the temptation to keep each other warm proves overwhelming. Dealing with unexpected feelings is hard enough, but what about an unexpected pregnancy? They're about to find out...

#2434 ONE SECRET NIGHT, ONE SECRET BABY
Moonlight Beach Bachelors • by Charlene Sands
Though Hollywood heartthrob Dylan McKay has no memory of that fateful night with his sister's best friend, he must face the music. He's made her pregnant and will make her his bride. But soon the shocking, unforgettable truth emerges...

#2435 THE RANCHER'S MARRIAGE PACT
Texas Extreme • by Kristi Gold
Marrying his sexy interior designer is convenient enough for rich rancher Dallas Calloway. He'll get his inheritance and she'll get a new lease on life. Then the business arrangement turns into more than they bargain for...

#2436 HIS SECRETARY'S SURPRISE FIANCÉ
Bayou Billionaires • by Joanne Rock
Winning at any cost might work on the football field, but will demanding a fake engagement really keep billionaire sportsman Dempsey Reynaud's alluring assistant in his life?

YOU CAN FIND MORE INFORMATION ON UPCOMING HARLEQUIN® TITLES,
FREE EXCERPTS AND MORE AT WWW.HARLEQUIN.COM.

HDCNM0216

REQUEST YOUR FREE BOOKS!
2 FREE NOVELS PLUS 2 FREE GIFTS!

HARLEQUIN®

Desire

ALWAYS POWERFUL, PASSIONATE AND PROVOCATIVE

YES! Please send me 2 FREE Harlequin® Desire novels and my 2 FREE gifts (gifts are worth about $10). After receiving them, if I don't wish to receive any more books, I can return the shipping statement marked "cancel." If I don't cancel, I will receive 6 brand-new novels every month and be billed just $4.55 per book in the U.S. or $5.24 per book in Canada. That's a savings of at least 13% off the cover price! It's quite a bargain! Shipping and handling is just 50¢ per book in the U.S. and 75¢ per book in Canada.* I understand that accepting the 2 free books and gifts places me under no obligation to buy anything. I can always return a shipment and cancel at any time. Even if I never buy another book, the two free books and gifts are mine to keep forever.

225/326 HDN GH2P

Name _____ (PLEASE PRINT) _____

Address _____ Apt. # _____

City _____ State/Prov. _____ Zip/Postal Code _____

Signature (if under 18, a parent or guardian must sign) _____

Mail to the **Reader Service:**
IN U.S.A.: P.O. Box 1867, Buffalo, NY 14240-1867
IN CANADA: P.O. Box 609, Fort Erie, Ontario L2A 5X3

Want to try two free books from another line?
Call 1-800-873-8635 or visit www.ReaderService.com.

* Terms and prices subject to change without notice. Prices do not include applicable taxes. Sales tax applicable in N.Y. Canadian residents will be charged applicable taxes. Offer not valid in Quebec. This offer is limited to one order per household. Not valid for current subscribers to Harlequin Desire books. All orders subject to credit approval. Credit or debit balances in a customer's account(s) may be offset by any other outstanding balance owed by or to the customer. Please allow 4 to 6 weeks for delivery. Offer available while quantities last.

Your Privacy—The Reader Service is committed to protecting your privacy. Our Privacy Policy is available online at www.ReaderService.com or upon request from the Reader Service.

We make a portion of our mailing list available to reputable third parties that offer products we believe may interest you. If you prefer that we not exchange your name with third parties, or if you wish to clarify or modify your communication preferences, please visit us at www.ReaderService.com/consumerschoice or write to us at Reader Service Preference Service, P.O. Box 9062, Buffalo, NY 14240-9062. Include your complete name and address.

HDI5

Claire looked completely panicked by the thought of
Luca having access to her child.

Their child.

It seemed so wrong for him to have a child with a
woman he'd never met. But now that he had a living,
breathing daughter, he wasn't about to sit back and
pretend it didn't happen. Eva was probably the only child
he would ever have, and he'd already missed months of
her life. That would not continue.

"We can and we will." Luca spoke up at last. "Eva
is my daughter, and I've got the paternity test results to
prove it. There's not a judge in the county of New York
who won't grant me emergency visitation while we await
our court date. They will say when and where and how
often you have to give her to me."

Claire sat, her mouth agape at his words. "She's just
a baby. She's only six months old. Why fight me for her
just so you can hand her over to a nanny?"

Luca laughed at her presumptuous tone. "What makes
you so certain I'll have a nanny for her?"